I0666927

They Should've Told You At The Door

You At The Door

S.W. Campbell

Published by Shawn Campbell

They Should've Told You At The Door

Copyright © 2025 by Shawn Campbell
All rights reserved. Printed in the United States of America
No part of this book may be used or reproduced in any manner
whatsoever without written permission except in the case of brief
quotations embodied in critical articles and reviews.

ISBN: 979-8-9870287-8-0

To Mallory and Azilynn, the best things in my life.

They Should've Told You At The Door

Table of Contents

They Should've Told You At The Door

Preface

Looking back at the stories in this collection, written between November of 2016 and July of 2018, it's plain to see that this was the height of my literary output, though more in quantity than quality. This is not to say that the stories in this collection are not well worth reading, only that I was becoming more easily distracted by other projects. In each of the years of 2016, 2017, and 2018, my writing output was over 225,000 words each year, but less than half of that was towards the writing of short stories and novels, the lion-share instead being focused on books about family history and a comedic history blog called Professor Errare.

In retrospect the shift towards these other literary outlets makes a lot of sense. Being a weekly blog, Professor Errare provided a much more consistent source of dopamine hits provided by Facebook likes and comments by friends. Started as a way to help people process the first election of Donald Trump, by pointing out how every president had been a jackass in their own unique way, it became a humorous outlet for my own frustrations, albeit one that sucked away a lot of time and energy. As for the family history books, they combined my love of history with the importance of knowing about one's family imbued in me by my late grandmother, culminating in an annual Christmas present to various family members.

In comparison, my more traditional literary endeavors were hitting roadblock after frustrating roadblock. The decision to self-publish my first novel, The Uncanny Valley, in 2016 had been a difficult one, and my attempts at self-marketing did little to help. Even worse, though I knew I wanted to begin writing a second novel, I repeatedly found myself floundering in actually doing so. I came up with ideas for numerous books, and even started writing a couple, but in all I failed to keep up the needed momentum. The first was a novella about deer called The Wild Ones, which in turn gave way to a novel about a past relationship that was to be called The Knight On The Gelded Pony, which went nowhere as well. Finding the former uninteresting and the latter too personal, I then shifted to a third attempt, a novel about suburbia called The Owl Sees All.

I had first come up with the idea for The Owel Sees All soon after finishing The Uncanny Valley, writing a complete outline one night while visiting my brother. Focused on trying to get The Uncanny Valley published, I put it aside until picking it back up again for further refinement in late 2016. Unfortunately, like the previous two attempts it did not go anywhere, but what it did do was set me to writing a short story about a young man in the Peace Corps living in the Caribbean, which then morphed into a novella, and then eventually my second novel. Entitled Papaya, it would not be finished until mid-2018.

During this same period, the writing and submission of short stories became increasingly more like a second job rather than a hobby, a situation only exacerbated by the weekly release schedule of Professor Errare and the Christmas deadline of the family history books. Between November of 2016 and July of

2018, I wrote a total of 49 short stories and made 4,454 submissions to various literary reviews and journals, averaging around 212 per month. While this did result in nine publications on top of my previous ten publications, including in the well-known Tin House, it was a constant grind which looking back I'm not sure how I kept up for as long as I did.

In the end, this period of time ended much the way it began, with self-publication. In the early part of 2018, I self-published a collection of 36 of my earliest short stories which I entitled An Unsated Thirst, both for the general collective sense of those stories and for the lack of the literary success I craved. It was bittersweet. Sales were limited to friends and family and more people preferred the two collections of Professor Errare posts I released, 45 Jerks and Counting self-published in 2016 and 40 American Jackasses self-published in 2017.

Looking back over the short stories in this collection, it is interesting to note the trends. For one thing, many stories during this period began to become quirkier and stranger compared to their predecessors, something especially prevalent in the shorter pieces. While I've always had what one would call a weird sense of humor and a tendency to take a joke too far, it was a trait which had been relatively restrained in my earlier writings. In comparison, this was much less the case in the snarky style in which I wrote as Professor Errare, and in hindsight it is obvious this made it much more okay to loosen up in my more literary endeavors as well. Of interest, three of the five stories in this collection which were published by literary reviews were of this stranger bent (The Devil, Nickels and Dimes, and A Public Service Announcement), something I would not come to appreciate until much later.

Another interesting tidbit is this is also the first collection to involve multiple what could better be described as short essays rather than short stories, exploring various themes from serious world events, to personal experiences, to more light-hearted

3

japes. Though there are of course many examples of similar types of writing in my earlier collections, especially the ones covering my earliest writings in 2013 and prior, such breaks from fiction were more focused on singular themes, and again I probably have to credit my time doing Professor Errare as the catalyst for being more adventuresome in trying this type of writing. As an aside, many of these short essays began their lives as Facebook posts which I enjoyed enough to save from the ever growing depths of my Facebook timeline. Perhaps saving them was a bit of self-indulgence, but I still enjoy reading many of them today.

The combination of the above makes this short story collection perhaps one of the more disjointed of the ones I have released so far, but in that I also find it to be one of the more interesting. For those who read it and know me, little of the random strangeness will be that much of a surprise, which is why I gave it the title They Should've Told You At The Door. It's either that or just because I like how it sounds. I can't quite remember.

With all that being said, I'll end with the usual disclaimer that these stories and essays contain pieces of lots of different people, some of which you may recognize. However, fictional characters are almost always amalgamations of many different people, and even when they're not, they only represent short windows from a specific point of view. We're all just a bunch of hyper-intelligent apes doing the best we can on a speck of dust in the cosmos. Happy reading.

Nickels and Dimes

Donald had a total of three shopping carts. The whole affair moved like a caterpillar. Donald would push the front cart ten feet forward, run back for the second, push it forward, and then run back again for the third. In this way he moved slowly and surely through the long green space of the park towards the bench where Douglas sat. The cartwheels rattled on the sidewalk seams, every jostle eliciting the tinny sound of clinking aluminum. The three carts were filled to overflowing with black and white garbage bags stuffed full of cans. In the basket, hanging from the sides, and piled high on top. Strange postmodernist mushrooms of waste, held together by plastic, tape, string, and rotting bungee cords. Every now and again a rogue can would manage to escape from the confines of one of the bags, dropping to the ground, a sudden flash of bright color in a world beginning to fade to grays and browns. Donald would quickly scoop it up and shove it back into the collection.

It took close to twenty minutes from the time Douglas first saw him for Donald to get close. Douglas didn't mind. It was a nice distraction from watching Lane across the way, thirty feet or so, sitting on his own bench beneath the big oak tree, covering himself with a tarp so nobody could see him injecting himself. Lane had needs that weren't all that fun to watch. It was starting to get cold out. Not as cold as it was going to be later in the year, but there was definitely starting to be a chill. Douglas didn't like thinking about it. Donald and his antics were a welcome distraction.

The first two carts pulled up alongside. Donald mumbled to himself as he moved, his eyes darting from cart to cart, trying to keep them all in sight at once. Donald was always mumbling to himself, a never ending leaking of air. He crinkled with every step, a light rustling from the newspaper shoved into his greasy windbreaker and pants. A brown knit cap with a hole in it was pulled low over his ears. Douglas cleared his throat and gave a holler.

"What the hell you doing?"

Donald's head shot forward like a dog that heard its name. His whole body tensed.

"My fucking cans."

Douglas let out a laugh that fell into a hacking cough. Donald watched, ready for anything. Douglas recovered and laughed again.

"I don't want none of your cans you damn loon. Haven't seen you in a while. Where you been?"

Donald didn't answer. He stood warily, his head jerking between Douglas on the bench and the rearmost shopping cart still ten feet behind. Douglas snorted and spit before asking his question again.

"I said where you been?"

Donald jogged back to get his third cart, throwing a hasty answer over his shoulder.

"Busy."

"I can see that."

Donald pushed the third cart up with its mates then faced Douglas. He was sweating despite the cold. He kept one hand back on the plastic of the bags, assuring himself that the whole collection wouldn't just disappear. They stayed that way for a bit until Donald accepted that it was his turn to speak.

"What are you doing?"

"Same as always, just sitting on this bench, waiting for the mission to reopen."

Donald nodded. The mission always kicked everyone out during the day. It was only a place to stay at night. Douglas snorted and spit again.

"Haven't seen you there in a while."

"Been busy."

"Obviously. You must have a couple thousand cans there."

Donald's posture got defensive again.

"They're my fucking cans."

"Relax. They're your cans. I ain't no thief."

Donald relaxed again, at least slightly. He still fidgeted, but Donald always fidgeted. Douglas lifted a paper sack from between his feet and gestured with it towards Donald.

"You want a drink?"

Donald bit his lip. A hand shot up and scratched fiercely at his head along the side of his knit cap.

"Mission don't like it when you get all slobbery."

He was right. The mission didn't like it when you got totally wrecked. Such people were more liable to cause trouble. Sometimes if you were too wrecked, they wouldn't let you in.

"It's just a forty. Plus, I'm only sipping."

Donald looked back at his carts and then craned his neck to get a better look around the park.

"Who's that under the tarp?"

"Just Lane."

"What he doing?"

"His usual junk. Same as always."

7

"Fucking government rainbows."

"Yep."

Not everything Donald said made a lot of sense, it was easier just to go along with it. Douglas gestured with the paper sack at the empty portion of his bench.

"Take a load off. Be nice to have someone to talk to for a bit."

"Pretty busy."

"Just for a while. C'mon, take a bit of a break with me."

Donald craned his neck all around again before steering his eyes back to the bottle.

"Okay."

Douglas waited patiently while Donald used bungee cords to tie the three carts together. When he finally sat down, Douglas unscrewed the cap on the bottle in the bag and passed it over. Donald took it and eyed it carefully.

"What kind you got?"

"Colt 45."

"Lando's favorite."

"Yep."

Donald took a sip and passed it back. Douglas wiped the rim with his hand and took a drink himself. A little dribbled down into his whiskers.

"So, what's all the cans for?"

"They're my fucking cans."

"I know. You ought to turn them in, be easier than hauling them around everywhere."

"Can't turn them in yet."

Douglas took another drink from the bottle and tried to pass it back to Donald, but Donald shook his head. Douglas shrugged and sipped again before replacing the cap and putting the bottle back between his feet.

"Why the hell not?"

"Don't you read the paper?"

Donald was smiling. Douglas hated it when Donald smiled. He had some pretty ganked up teeth.

"No professor. I haven't been reading the paper."

Donald unzipped his windbreaker slightly and rooted around amongst the wadded newspapers in his jacket. Finally finding what he wanted he yanked it out, smoothed it on his knee, and passed it over.

"They're doubling the deposit next week."

Douglas looked at the newspaper page. It was the Sunday comics. He studied it intently for a moment, reading Beetle Bailey then Blondie, before handing it back.

"No shit?"

Donald wadded back up the newspaper and put it back in his jacket.

"No shit."

Douglas sat back and stared at the three carts. Donald picked his nose and flicked something into the grass.

"I'm going to buy a nice coat. Something thick and waterproof. I ain't going to freeze this winter."

Douglas needed a little time to think. He reached down between his legs and picked back up the paper bag covered bottle. He unscrewed the lid and took a good healthy pull to get the synapses firing. A forty of Colt 45 cost $1.89, or thirty-eight cans. In a week it would only be nineteen. It was hard to think. Donald kept yammering on.

"Then I'm going to buy a nice pair of gloves, and maybe a new hat, then maybe some new boots. Definitely some wool socks. Some nice wool socks. Warm. Then....."

Douglas cut in with a wave of his hand.

"It don't make no sense. Who the hell going to be throwing away all those dimes?"

"What do you mean who's going to be throwing away all those dimes? Same damn people that's been throwing away all the damn nickels."

9

Douglas took another drink from his bottle. The gears were turning now. He just needed to keep them lubricated.

"I just can't see as many people throwing out dimes as throwing out nickels."

Donald was frowning now. He was trying to sort it out but was out of his element. Douglas powered forward to drive his point home.

"Look, do you find more cans east of 82nd or west of 82nd?"

"West of 82nd."

"And why is that?"

"Because the people east have less money."

"Exactly, those nickels are more valuable to them. So more of them keep their cans."

"So?"

"So what happens when they're dimes instead of nickels? More people are going to be keeping their cans if they're worth dimes."

Douglas took another drink. Donald's face was scrunched up in concentration.

"Not all the people are going to start keeping their cans."

"Never said they would."

"Do you think twice as many are going to be keeping their cans?"

Douglas paused. He had to think about that one. One drink didn't do the trick, nor did two. It turned out to be a three drink question.

"I don't know. Probably not."

"Well there you go, still better off."

Donald went back to mumbling about all of the things he was going to buy once the deposit jumped up. Douglas went back to wetting his whistle, his brain whirling furiously in his head. The big old oak tree across the way creaked as it swayed in the breeze, its skeletal branches clawing at the gray wisps of clouds lumbering their way across the blue sky. Two joggers ran by

10

with a dog in a coat, swerving deep into the grass to avoid Donald's shopping carts on the sidewalk. The dog stopped and let out a bark at the two men on the bench, but its masters pulled it back around. Douglas made a face at it as they jogged away.

"I don't know. If you get a fancy coat ain't someone just going to beat your ass for it?"

Donald was smiling again with his ganky smile.

"No man, you don't get it, we'll all have nice coats. We're all going to be getting dimes."

Douglas drank again. The bottle was getting close to empty. Everyone having more money. What could be wrong with that? Hell, if a forty only cost nineteen cans he wouldn't have to spend so much time scrounging to get another one. There'd be more time for sitting around, or if he kept working just as much, more money in his pocket. A nice new coat. That didn't sound too bad. It would be a hell of a lot better than the two sweatshirts he was currently wearing. Something nicer than the crap that got donated to the mission.

"I don't know. It doesn't make much sense."

"No, just think about it. Not only do we get coats. We get tents and sleeping bags. Be nice to have a warm tent and sleeping bag. We could tell those assholes at the mission to shove it up their asses. No more jerks coming around with their bibles. No more people telling us what to do and when to do it. I'm talking financial freedom man. Middle finger to the man. Everyone man. Fucking everyone."

Donald was really on a tear now. Something was nibbling at the back of Douglas' mind. It all sounded nice. It all sounded too good to be true.

"It just doesn't make sense."

Donald looked annoyed.

"How does it not make any damn sense?"

"Won't more people move here if we're all making dimes when they're making nickels?"

"Yeah so?"

Douglas tipped back the bottle and swallowed the last dregs in the bottom. Across the way Lane and the tarp hiding him rolled off the bench and onto the ground. Lane lay there, not moving except for the occasional erratic shallow breath. Donald didn't seem to notice. Douglas laid the empty bottle in its bag in between them on the bench.

"Just think about the inflation."

The Volunteer

Sheila sat on the log of a fallen palm tree and waited. It was hot and she was sweating, but there was nothing that could be done about it. The sound of the ocean crashing against the shore emanated from the other side of the tree line. Maybe she'd walk back the mile to JoJo's on the beach rather than on the road. It would be a nice walk. All of the beaches of Vieques were beautiful.

The woman had said two o'clock. Sheila pulled out her phone and checked the time. The woman was already half an hour late. Sheila took in a breath and let it out. Punctuality was important but given the circumstances it was understandable. For a moment Sheila couldn't remember the woman's name. She had heard so many over the past few weeks that they had all gotten jumbled together. Alondra. That was it. Alondra Madera. In truth, Sheila didn't mind the wait. Her arms and shoulders were sore from all the hard work over the past few days. She got sore a lot easier now that she was in her forties. It was also difficult to find time for oneself at JoJo's with every square inch of floor space covered in sleeping bags. There

13

wasn't even enough room to do any yoga, never mind the shower situation.

A male frigatebird landed on the other side of the log. It was dark black with a green sheen and a bright red throat. Sheila knew it was a frigatebird because one of the locals had pointed it out to her. She sat perfectly still. The frigatebird cocked its head, swinging about its long hooked beak, looking at her with one dark eye. Its red throat pouch inflated, signaling it was looking for a mate. Sheila was flattered but didn't think it would probably work out. She smiled at her own joke. The bird must have been less entertained. It beat its wings and flew off back toward the ocean.

Alondra what was her name still had not arrived. Sheila checked her phone again. It had been less than five minutes since the last time she had checked. Sheila scrolled through her apps and tapped on the one marked *Photos*. She flicked through the pictures, deleting some and mentally noting others. They were all pictures of everybody working. There was Frank hammering nails on a new tin roof. There was her running a chainsaw to cut up a tree not that different from the one she was sitting on, though the one she currently occupied hadn't fallen through somebody's roof. It was a good picture. She let herself admit it to herself. There was JoJo, with his long raven hair, talking to the house's owner. The owner was a fat woman, skin like dark leather, hair the color of steel wool. A worn dress hid any signs of her ample figure. In the first picture she was smiling at JoJo. In the second she was unsmiling, staring at the camera out of the corner of her eye. Sheila deleted the second photo. She continued scrolling, deleting some and mentally choosing which others she would post as soon as she had a chance. Service was still pretty spotty. JoJo had a booster at the house, but even then it was agonizingly slow. They still hadn't gotten all the towers working yet.

A red jeep came down the gravel road. It came to a halt just a few feet from the log. Alondra got out. She was a short local woman with hair dyed a light brown with blonde streaks. In her office she had worn a skirt and pumps. Out here she wore jeans and tennis shoes, which made her done up hair and earrings seem out of place. The bracelets on her wrist jangled as she hopped to the ground.

"Sorry for being late. My husband insisted I take the jeep if I was going to come out here, and then I got stuck behind one of the big utility power trucks, you know, it was a whole thing." Alondra shook herself a little and regained her composure. "Anyways, so good to see you again."

Sheila put her phone away and smiled.

"Good to see you again too." She gestured at the log in the road. "I'm guessing we walk from here?"

Alondra flashed another one of her winning smiles. She had a grin full of bright white teeth except for one front tooth turning slightly brown, which Sheila did her best not to stare at.

"It's not up much farther. It won't be hard to get somebody to clear it away later. You know, but things have been so busy of late."

Alondra accentuated the statement with a twist of her wrist in the air, jangling her bracelets again. She gave a little laugh which Sheila answered with a forced smile. The tree in the road was understandable. Things like that happened after a hurricane. Alondra crawled over the log and started walking down the road, Sheila following in her wake.

The house at the end of the road wasn't much larger than the one Sheila had been working at earlier that day, maybe nine hundred square feet. Its walls were painted a brilliant cyan blue, though they were chipping, exposing layers of white, yellow, and the concrete underneath it all. Alondra clucked to herself as she unlocked the door. She swept in and started opening windows to let in the ocean air. One of the windows was broken, the glass lying shattered along the floor. Everything in the interior was concrete. Concrete floors, concrete walls, and concrete counters. Living room, kitchen, two bedrooms, and a bathroom. Other than an old musty couch and some random pieces of garbage it was empty. It seemed so spacious compared to the cramped confines of JoJo's house. Alondra opened the last window and spun back to Sheila with a warm smile.

"So, what brought you to Vieques? Bad time to be a tourist."

Alondra did the little spinning motion again with her wrist. Sheila tried to ignore the nonchalant attitude. It seemed inappropriate given how bad the hurricane had been.

"I'm part of a volunteer group. Making It Better. We bring volunteers over to help repair houses owned by low income people."

Alondra smiled.

"This is certainly the area for it."

There was a strange hint of something in the other woman's tone that Sheila didn't like, but she ignored it as she stood a little straighter.

"I'm actually the brand manager for a large property management firm in Seattle."

Alondra kept smiling.

"How nice. My brother runs a contracting firm."

Sheila felt momentarily confused, but Alondra pushed forward before she puzzled it out.

"Anyway, feel free to look around. My contacts think this area will have water again in about two weeks and electricity in a month. Not ideal, but pretty good considering it's only been two months since, well, you know."

Alondra twirled her wrist again. Sheila felt her hands involuntarily curl into fists but forced them to reopen.

"My friend JoJo said solar panels would probably be a good idea. Do you know what the Sun Index is here?"

Alondra looked slightly puzzled, but she hid it well.

"It gets very sunny here."

Sheila started walking around the gray world of the house. It looked rough, but it had potential. Concrete might look drab, but it made for a sturdy structure. The roof had a few leaks, but those could be fixed. A little paint and maybe some tile would really spruce up the place. Hell, if someone had some money to put into it, they could make it pretty nice. Alondra was in the kitchen, checking her phone. When she saw Sheila approach she instantly snapped back into her persona.

"Well, what do you think?"

"It looks pretty good."

"Perfect."

The two women fell silent. Sheila put her hands on her hips and turned a slow circle. She saw Alondra drop her smile out of the corner of her eye but raise it again when the other woman came back into view. Alondra tapped the concrete counter with a finger.

"So is your group buying for more space for your volunteers?"

Sheila shook her head.

"Oh no, I'm buying it for myself. I got here two weeks ago and just fell in love with the island. I have a vacation home just outside Miami, but I'm going to sell it. Out here is just so much more authentic." For just a moment the mask that was Alondra's face fell away, but only for a millisecond. A short burst of distaste that seemed more imagined than real. Sheila shrugged. "Pretty spur of the moment, I know."

Alondra smiled warmly.

"It's a good time to buy. Lots of motivated sellers in this area."

Sheila smiled.

"I'll take it."

Alondra nodded.

"Good. I'll go back to my office and get the paperwork put together. These things take a bit more time than normal, but I'm sure I can get the bank to push it through faster."

Sheila was beaming. She felt light, almost ready to float right off the ground in her giddiness.

"Excellent. Thank you. Do you know anything about shipping furniture over from the mainland?"

Alondra's smile was becoming more intense.

"There's shipping services. Pretty expensive right now, you know, because of the...."

Alondra twisted her wrist in the air again, jangling her bracelets. Sheila didn't even notice. She was too happy to be perturbed about anything.

"It's no problem. I have the money."

The Shadow In The Light

Working on day three of a cold. One of the worst things about being sick is the social isolation as you try to get better and avoid getting others sick. Your mind starts playing tricks on you.

While laying in my bed in the darkness I notice a faint band of light on the far wall from the narrow window above my head. The light comes from a front porch light on the house across the street from my backside neighbors, everything just perfectly lined up to allow it to shine on the wall in front of me each night.

Tonight, I notice that the light on the wall goes dark from left to right. It stays that way for a bit but then comes back. It almost looks like a shape trying to peak in. Ridiculous I know, but when you're alone in bed, already weakened by a cold, weird thoughts enter your head, and slivers of doubt are allowed to take hold.

The shadow comes again. I raise my arm. The shadow disappears suddenly, leaving just the thin darkened shape of my arm. I put my arm down and wait. After a minute the shadow returns. I raise my arm again and it disappears just as suddenly.

Now I'm left with a choice. I can rise up and look, see what there is to see, or stay in my bed, wrapped in the security of unknowing. I'm not scared, just leery, a victim of a bored mind who knows that logic and statistics are on my side, but that statistics don't mean shit in an individual event.

I wait with bated breath. The shadow returns. I wiggle my feet under my blankets. The shadow does not react. I pull them slowly upwards without sitting up, willing hollows where my legs had once been to continue giving the impression that they're still there. I brace myself, ready to spring.

The shadow disappears. I wait. Ready. One minute. Two. I can feel every beat of my heart. My throat itches, but I dare not cough. I can see myself springing up. I can see a face in the darkness. I can feel myself thrown back in surprise and fright, reaching for my phone with panicked fingers. The shadow returns. It seems to peak in, pull back, and then return for a better look. I throw myself upwards, ready to go face to face with whatever may be outside.

There's nothing. The distant light shines unencumbered. No branches or shrubs nearby to block its path. I stare out the window, waiting, but nothing changes. I lay back down. I raise up my arm and move its shadow through the light. Yes, it is coming from the narrow window. I wave my hand and the shadow appears and disappears, almost as if it's waving back. It's a little unnerving. The floor creaks and I feel a small shot of adrenaline. Nothing. Just the house settling. I wave my hand across the light again. The shadow repeats as well. Part of me wants to say hello, but I don't, that would be ridiculous.

I scrunch lower in my bed, allowing me to see sky through the window. I wait, my head swiveling between the window and the light. I wait for a shadow that does not seem to want to come. I count the seconds. I grow bored after four minutes. I start to laugh at myself. What a fool I've been. Age thirty-four and acting like a child.

The shadow darkens the entire wall. It covers it like black ink. My head swings upwards towards the window. I can see all the glass clearly. There's nothing there. Just an angle of sky overhead. The shadow is still on the wall, mocking my inability to understand. Laughing at my futile attempts to comprehend the truth. I stop breathing. I don't move. The shadow retreats and I start to breathe again, but it whips back with a ferocity and flashes across the light once, twice, thrice. It's teasing me. Having fun at my expense. I hate it. Oh how I loathe it. I rise up in my bed and it's gone again, as quickly as if imagined. Part of me wants to say hello again, but I tell that part of me to shut the hell up. Something pops with a wooden bang in another part of my home. It's just the house settling. It's just the god damn house settling.

I lay my head back on my pillow. Enough is enough. I need to go to bed. I need my sleep to get better. I crack one eye open. The light is still on the far wall. I wait, but there is nothing. Just satisfying light glowing dimly in the distance. Overactive imagination. That is all. However, I cannot help but do one last test. One last piece of proof to lay it all to bed. I raise my arm. Nothing. Dark fingers wiggle in the light, dabbing in the golden pond. Nothing. I wave it back and forth. Nothing. Satisfied I lower it back down. The moment the last impression of a fingertip exits it returns. A horrible darkness more complete than the depths of the deepest cavern. A terrible stain upon peace and sanity.

I rise up and press my face against the window. Staring with all my might. Willing myself to see what is not there. How long I stood there I cannot say, but my skin grew cold, the last warmth from my blankets dissipating from my naked form into the darkness. Something must be there. We live in a world of logic damn it. There is nothing, just me mentally screaming into the night.

I see it. Just a glimpse which grips my heart in an icy hand. An ethereal form standing at the edge of darkness near the source of my dread and fears. A ghostly figure partially transparent. It's horrifying to see, but I cannot turn away. It stands half hidden by the darkness, but as I watch it emerges, raising forth a terrible arm to point, the light only partially filtering through its form which seems to shimmer and grow indistinct. I can see it there and I know the truth. I can know the terrible truth. I can see just the barest hint of the blood colored stripes where they let less light through. It's a flag, nothing more than a flag, occasionally floating on a breeze lighter than the softest touch.

I lay back down in my bed. The shadow skitters across the light on the wall and then retreats. The house creaks. I close my eyes. I'm thirty-four. I'm too old for this shit.

Appendix

I first noticed the pain while at dinner at my friend Eric's house. He was hosting a post holiday get together, a chance to catch up after the familial obligations. It wasn't a big group, just four couples and lonely old me. Eric had scored himself a spiral cut honey ham from a post Christmas bargain bin at the grocery store. It was only two more days until New Years, and few if any link a new beginning with spiral cut honey ham, regardless of how delicious it might be, but either way it seemed like a good enough reason to get together. Following dinner we lounged in the dining room, sipping drinks, swapping stories, and doing our best to ignore the shrill barking of Eric's rat dog. Are you picturing Eric as a burly man who works construction, the epitome of a caricature of a small town uncle? If not, then you are picturing him wrong. To help pass the time we were playing Cards Against Humanity, laughing at the smutty and horrifying combinations, most of which we had seen before, all fully aware that the entertainment value of the game had already passed its peak several months ago.

It was at this time that I first felt the pain. A small twist in my abdomen. Slight, but noticeable. Being a man of occasional gastric shifting and gaseous expulsion, I often fail to consume enough fiber, I gave it no mind. I had felt such pains before and they had never failed to work themselves out. Besides, the group's attention had shifted to a much more gleeful topic than the oft heard jokes printed on the cards in everybody's hands. Nikki had asked for the time, a strange request given that a clock hung on the wall not ten feet in front of her face.

"Can't you read that?"

"No"

"Jesus Christ."

Tests quickly followed. People leaning back and holding up fingers for her to count through squinted eyes. Heavy guffaws and friendly ribbing. We had all known her for years, but none of us had ever guessed such a thing. Here before us was a woman in her late twenties. A woman of high education and a comfortable living status. A woman who beyond all levels of chance, but for those created by willful stubbornness, was either extremely nearsighted or possibly illiterate. A few further tests dissuaded us from the latter, but did little to calm our laughter, or our fairly serious suggestion that she needed to get her eyes checked before she ran over someone with her car.

Whatever jokes followed I am uncertain, for it was then that the pain in my gut grew to a twisting knot. I politely excused myself and found my way to the commode on the same level, a small windowless room off the kitchen. Seating myself on the throne, my Herculean toe curling efforts were rewarded by a slow but steady series of hard singular plops that would have embarrassed a rabbit. Believing myself done, I did what was needed and rose but quickly sat again for an encore similar to the main show. This continued for about half an hour. I don't know if you've ever been trapped in such a situation, but if not, I can tell you that it is not a pleasant one, especially when you lack a phone or other reading materials to help pass the time. Given the circumstances you wouldn't think I would be bored, but I read the labels, in their entirety, of every cleaning product stored beneath the sink.

Not quite feeling finished, the plops had tapered off, but the occasional pang of discomfort continued to cross my mid-section, I nonetheless relented and returned to the outside world. The embarrassment of my long absence had overcome my feeling that I was leaving a job not quite done. My friends of course said nothing, which had more to do with the general feeling that the party was winding down, rather than my friends' belief in an etiquette where one does not give somebody the business for being in the bathroom for too long. Things lasted for about half an hour more and then began to drift apart as they do. Drinks were finished, empty offers to help clean up were politely refused, coats were donned, goodbyes were stated, and we all went on our way. It was only around 10:30, but my friend Eric lived clear out in the suburbs, and most of us faced a half hour drive or more back home.

The moment I closed my car door I knew there was going to be trouble. The pain in my gut shifted and intensified, building an urgent sense that I would soon need to seclude myself once again. This of course left me with an uncertain choice. Either start driving and hope for the best or expose myself to the shame of knocking on my friend's door and demanding re-entry to use their bathroom for an indefinite amount of time. Since I was in a state of disquiet, not alarm, I chose the former and started the long drive home. Every green light was a blessing and every red light was a curse. I think it goes without saying that I drove more aggressively than what would be considered an acceptable norm. The pain went in waves like the ocean, some big and some small, rising and subsiding, but all slowly working their way towards high tide. The car hit nearly ninety on the freeway, something I excused with the hypothesis that even the most hardline traffic cop would have a difficult time giving a ticket to a man who had just defecated in his pants. Luckily, I never had to find out.

Things were at full alarm when I roared into my driveway, and of course my hands chose that moment to be clumsy in the unlocking of my front door, but I managed to get to my sanctuary just in the nick of time, only to be greeted again by the singular hard plops, similar to slowly dropping chocolate chips one at a time. This result was less than satisfactory. I stayed on the toilet for about an hour, long periods of rest followed by a flurry of activity which involved much effort, but little reward. During one period of rest, I shuffled out to get a book to read, and in another, I shuffled again to turn up the heat, rushing by my front windows in horror of someone choosing that time to look in. I stayed so long that my legs fell asleep, so they burned as though on fire when I finally rose. Things still did not feel quite right, but wanting sleep, I brushed my teeth and found my way to bed.

This sequence of events repeated itself several times throughout the night. Each time the pain and discomfort woke me from my slumber, and each time I dazedly made my way to the bathroom to continue the war within, vowing to improve my diet. The campaign was not going in my favor. Not only was the pain getting worse, but I was working more for lower yields. This was a bit disconcerting. As mentioned earlier, I had been through such gastrointestinal malaise many times before, and the steps were not unknown to me. The rise, the peak, and the fall. Things were decidedly still on the uphill side.

The pain was something worth describing. At times I felt perfectly fine, but at others I would double over, unable to unfold, screaming obscenities which echoed off the uncaring grimy tiles. Imagine someone sticking a poor drill in your gut, but instead of cutting a clean hole, it instead grabs on and twists everything into an ever tightening mess, the electric motor bogging down with the effort. To say the least, it wasn't comfortable. The few moments I had in bed were filled with fitful sleep and worry for when the pain would come again.

The third time I rose to do battle was when I decided that the use of medical aides was in order. However, a quick search of my cupboards proved unsatisfactory at best. I found a thing of Tums, which weren't really made to solve my present problem, but I took a few anyways just for good measure. Near the back of the cupboard there was a bottle of bright pink Pepto Bismol, but I was loathe to try it given that the expiration date was from three years ago and the fact that the contents had solidified into a bright pink putty like substance. The last option was the bag of epsom salt on the top shelf, a method that I had heard of from the depths of the more senior members of our society, but one that I had never tried myself. I normally used the salts when I soaked my knee in the tub, I have long had a troublesome knee but had never considered the other uses printed on the label. However, not really in a position to be conservative regarding trying new things, I drank a glass of epsom salt mixed with water and then had a second just to be sure.

I was becoming increasingly worried over the growing pain in my gut. Already it had surpassed my normal experience, and it was giving no signs of letting up. There was a growing worry that it might be something more serious, perhaps an impacted bowel, or something of similar unpleasantness. I had not been able to pass anything for some time, but the feeling of needing to had only grown. The first thoughts that maybe I should go to the hospital entered my head, but running counter was the fear that I would get there only to discover there was nothing wrong beyond a little constipation. Nobody wants to be that guy, wasting precious medical resources on a little bit of tummy trouble. These worries were somewhat muted by a sudden wracking pain which not only doubled me over, but toppled me from my throne, leaving me writhing on my bathmat, doing my

27

best to choke back the bile rising in my throat. The pain fell
back, but kept throbbing, and while noticing how filthy the floor
was behind my toilet, I decided that a hospital visit was in order.
For a moment I considered calling an ambulance but quickly
abandoned the idea as both frivolous and wasteful.

I looked up the nearest hospital on my phone and chose the
one closest to the freeway. It made no difference to me, but it
seemed prudent given that at some point, being unencumbered
by relationships, I would have to call my mother and let her
know what was going on, a thought that I did not relish given the
amount of worry such a late night call would involve. It was
three in the morning. Unable to get myself to straighten out,
hunched over like an old man, I got dressed, got in my car,
adjusted my mirrors to my new stature, and started driving. It
was about sixty blocks to the hospital. Sixty blocks of traffic
lights and stop signs, a few of which I ran when nobody was
around. Halfway there the pain let up and the old fear returned
again. I nearly relented and turned back home, but a sudden
twinge kept me going forward.

For some, this innate need to refuse to go to the hospital may
seem strange, but perhaps I can make it more clear. Prior to the
current adventure, the worst pain I had ever felt had been when I
was living in Drumheller, in Alberta, Canada about five years
before. The pain at that time had been from the right side of my
gut down to where the front of my right leg attached to the rest
of me. After putting up with it for a couple of days, I had finally
relented and gone to see a doctor. Now while it is certainly true
that healthcare is free in Canada, getting it is another matter. If
you don't have a regular doctor, for which the waiting lists are
several years long, then every visit is an emergency room visit,
where you get whatever you happen to get. In my case, after a
three hour wait, I got a hunched back bony old man with a salt
and pepper beard down to his middle. The examination involved
me taking off my pants and letting this ancient relic run his

gnarled hands over me, his rheumy eyes pressed close, before announcing that while most of his experience had been in treating gonorrhea during the Korean War, he was pretty sure I just had a pulled muscle and needed to quit being such a baby. It later turned out he was probably right.

Upon arrival at the hospital, a multi-story multi-building edifice that leered over the freeway, I found myself with a conundrum. Having never been to this hospital before, I had no idea where the hell anything was. With the insistent stabbing pain in my gut goading me into action, I left my confusion behind and just parked my car in the first parking garage I saw, having to go to the third level since the first two were reserved for doctors. My coat felt heavy around my bent shoulders as I rode the elevator down and exited to the outside world. It was dark, it was cold, and it was raining. Short on options, I started making my way around the perimeter, searching for the emergency room, which I was hopefully guessing was somewhere nearby. Spoiler alert. It wasn't.

After approximately fifteen minutes of wandering around the hospital, bent over in pain, trying any door I saw to get in, I finally found the emergency room door on the opposite side of the complex from where I had parked. There were two ways I could go. The long way followed the sidewalk along the street, turning ninety degrees at the corner. The much shorter way was down a muddy landscaped hillside that ended close to the sliding glass door. Shivering, my eyes half filled with tears, I chose the more direct route.

It was slicker than it looked. I quickly found myself half walking and half sliding downward, gripping futilely at bushes and ferns to keep my feet, my hands filled with ripped away leaves. By some miracle I never fell, and I reached the bottom with muddy cuffs and shoes, but nothing else. However, much to my horror, I discovered something that could not be seen from above. The muddy slope did not end at the asphalt, but rather at a retaining wall six feet high. I looked back up the hill I had just come down, tracing the path of destruction I had created, realizing there was no way in hell I was ever going to make it back up. Climbing down was not an option either. My body was still folded over in pain. Seeing no other way, I laid down on the top of the retaining wall and rolled over the side, dropping to the pavement below.

Rising, bruised and battered, I limped towards the welcoming lights before me. The automatic doors whooshed open with a beep. The tired woman at the front desk gave me a cursory appraising glance.

"You look like you're in a lot of pain."

"Yeah."

"Fill out these forms."

I did as I was instructed and handed the clipboard back. We stood there for a moment. Me, holding out the clipboard as my gut sucked the rest of me inward towards it. Her, concentrating on her computer screen and moving her mouse in a way that suggested solitaire more than spreadsheets. Finally tiring of the game, I dropped the clipboard with a clatter, forcing the receptionist to turn enough of her attention to me to elicit a vague waving towards the chair filled lobby.

"Go sit down and wait until your name is called."

"Will it be long?"

The receptionist shrugged. The lobby was almost empty, which filled me with hope that it wouldn't be that long. I looked at the other patients with interest. I had never been in a hospital waiting room at three in the morning before. A harried looking woman, her hair sticking out at odd angles, held a squalling toddler, an ice pack wrapped in an old t-shirt pressed firmly to the child's hand. A big fat man sat next to the side of the TV, nobody sitting near, all scared off by the deep guttural coughs that occasionally shook his entire body, flapping his lips wildly as spittle ejected itself up to ten feet in front of him. An older gentleman sat with a woman that I assumed was his wife, though one can never tell, and it really wasn't any of my business either way, leaning back, his body rigid, moaning again and again about his leg. To be fair, the man was holding his leg as straight as possible, though not straight enough to hide the fact that it was bending the wrong way. The final person was an unsmiling man wearing sunglasses sitting alone in the corner. I'm not sure if he was a patient or just hanging out.

A nurse came out. The woman and the toddler of course got to go first, which might seem unfair to an observer, but seemed agreeable to everyone in the lobby in that with them gone the only noise was the sound of the TV, horrible phlegmy coughs, and the steady moaning of the man with the fucked up leg. I felt my chances of getting in second or third were pretty good. The man with the fucked up leg was probably ahead of me, but I probably looked worse than the others. After all, hadn't the receptionist mentioned how much I looked in pain? I thought about trying to read a magazine, the twisting in my gut wasn't so bad at the moment but decided against it. I didn't want anybody to think I wasn't in any pain. I didn't want to milk it or anything, but I didn't want to be passed over either.

A couple came in. The woman was in a nice dress, but she was limping and her long done up hair covered her face. It was obvious that at some point that day she had put a lot of work into it. The man was muscular, wearing a tracksuit. My hopes faded. They'd probably get in first. The woman brushed some of her hair back and I felt like a piece of shit. Her face looked terrible. Black eyes and bruises. Someone had worked her over. I tried to keep from looking, but my eyes followed them when they sat down. The man gave me a dirty look. Did he do it? Was he a remorseful piece of shit or just a good person trying to help out? I looked away. A nurse came out. The new couple got right in. The man with the fucked up leg doubled his moaning.

I tried to watch the TV, but it was hard with Coughy McCougherton hacking away right next to it. The pain in my gut intensified. I did my best to ignore it until it subsided back to more manageable levels. The sliding glass doors opened, ushering in a blast of cold air and an agitated girl with wild eyes accentuated by too much eyeliner. All eyes except the man in sunglasses followed her as she approached the receptionist. The receptionist gave the girl the up and down. The girl's hair was dyed jet black. Her clothes were dirty and torn. She couldn't stop fidgeting and her face kept tightening and twitching. She looked to be in her mid-twenties. All the elements were there for her to be attractive, but they were buried under her disheveled appearance.

"Is this the fucking hospital?"

The receptionist gave out a slight groan.

"Yes."

"I need to be committed."

"This isn't that type of hospital."

"Fuck!"

It was more of an explosion than a word. A guttural expulsion that echoed across the room.

"If I don't get committed I'm going to fucking kill myself."

The receptionist was unfazed.

"This isn't that type of hospital. If you want, I can give you directions to one."

"Fuck."

The girl pounded on the desk. The receptionist remained motionless, except for one hand which moved underneath the desk.

"I'm going to fucking kill myself."

"There isn't much we can do for you here."

The two women stared at each other. One with the crazed look of a cornered animal, the other with an apathy earned over years of dealing with such late night bullshit.

"Fuck."

"I can give you directions if you'd like."

The girl stared at the receptionist, breathing heavy. A phlegmy cough broke the silence. The girl licked her lips, looked back at the door, looked at the TV, and then back at the receptionist again.

"Where is it?"

"Salem."

"Fuck. How the hell am I supposed to get there?"

"I imagine there will be a bus in the morning."

The girl looked to be on the edge of tears. Her whole body was shaking.

"What the fuck am I supposed to do before then?"

The receptionist gestured towards the chairs.

"You can sit over there if you like."

The girl sat down and got out her phone, her foot rapidly tapping on the tile floor. She looked up and her eyes scanned the crowd. Everyone turned away, but I was a bit slow. The girl gave me an intense stare, flipped me off and went back to her phone. I went back to trying to watch the TV and hoping the nurse would soon come out to call my name. The old fear filled me again. Maybe it would be best if I just got up and went home. This was probably nothing. How embarrassing would it be to go to the hospital just to find out you're constipated?

It was about this time that the epsom salts began to take hold. At first, I couldn't tell the difference between the sudden new need and the aching pain that continued to roil my guts, but as the pressure built it quickly became apparent that this was slightly different. Something more within my realm of understanding. This new need created somewhat of an issue. On the one hand, I was worried that if I went to the bathroom it would be at that moment that the nurse came out to call my name. That's the way it always works. Everyone would probably assume that I had left. On the other, I certainly didn't want to poop my pants. For a short time I considered telling the receptionist I was going to go use the bathroom, but that just felt strange. Finally, I just gave in and did what I had to do. A part of me hoped that this final grand expulsion would solve the problem. However, in this I was disappointed.

When I returned to the lobby, both the girl and the moaning man with the fucked up leg were gone. The man in the sunglasses hadn't moved a muscle, and I began to be suspicious that maybe he was dead. I was concocting a plan to test this theory when a nurse came into the lobby. I leaned forward expectantly. She called out a name I didn't quite hear. Was it mine? The cougher got up, let loose one last phlegm filled explosion, and disappeared from my life forever. Fuck. The crazy girl came back in through the sliding glass doors and sat down. It had been nearly an hour since I had come in. The nurse came in again and said another barely audible name. Nobody moved. I perked up hopefully. The receptionist pointed at me. The nurse walked up.

"Are you Shawn?"

I looked up weakly, feeling pathetic, but at the same time not wanting to appear too healthy.

"Yes."

"C'mon."

The nurse led me back into a room filled with curtained off alcoves containing beds. She had me strip down and put on a hospital gown before poking and prodding me and asking various questions.

"Does it hurt here? How about it here? What if I do this?"

The nurse hemmed and hawed to herself, wrote a few things down, and left me sitting on the edge of the bed. I didn't feel that bad. The worry of a wasted trip was building. Across the way a large group of people were crowded around a bed, a spread from child to senior citizen. They were laughing and making jokes. The woman in the bed had a slightly pained look, but she was laughing too. A nurse came over to tell them that there were too many of them and that some would have to leave, but they laughed and ribbed her gently and the nurse started laughing with them. I felt decidedly lonely sitting half naked on my bed. The doctor came in and walked over, smelling of cigarettes and some kind of spray meant to hide the smell of cigarettes. The people across the way were laughing again. The doctor closed the curtain. He poked and prodded me in all the same places as the nurse. He asked all the same questions, then hemmed and hawed, wrote a few things down, and left. After a while a different nurse came in.

"How ya feeling?"

"Pretty shitty."

"We're going to run a sonogram in a bit to try and figure out what's wrong."

"Okay."

"Do you want anything for the pain?"

"Sure."

The nurse shoved a needle in my arm.

"We can't give you the good stuff until you have somebody here so we know you won't try to drive."

The nurse left. My guts tightened and almost burst. The electric screwdriver was futilely cranking away again. The sonogram guy popped in and wheeled me and my bed off without a word to a dark room where he hiked up my gown and rubbed goo on me. If I hadn't been in such pain this probably would have worried me more than it did. He ran his magic wand over the goo and laughed.

"Oops, used a little too much there."

I tried to smile weakly. The sonogram guy did his best to clean up the mess.

"Let me just get you another gown."

The sonogram guy helped me into my new gown and then wheeled me back to my alcove. After a bit the doctor came back in, leaving the curtain open, looked at my charts, and hemmed and hawed again.

"Inconclusive. Let's try that again."

I could see the nurse who brought me in from the lobby staring at me from across the room. It was not a friendly stare. What the fuck was that about? I got the strange sense that she thought I was lying to score free painkillers. It made me feel strangely guilty. Fuck her I thought, but I soon after forgave her. The painkillers were taking hold. I could still feel the throb, but it wasn't as intense as before. The people across the way were singing a song to someone they kept calling Tia. After a bit, a different sonogram guy came in, cracking jokes, and wheeled me and my bed off to the same dark room. He was a little less liberal with the goo. After finishing up, he wheeled me back to my alcove. The singing people across the way were gone, but the nurse from the lobby was still giving me the evil eye every time she passed. The doctor came back in and closed the curtain.

"Mr. Campbell?"

"Yes."

"Are you sure?"

"Certain."

"We think you have appendicitis, but both sonograms were inconclusive. We want to run a CAT scan to be sure."

"Okay."

"You might want to call someone."

"Okay."

The doctor left, leaving me in solitude. Someone on the other side of the curtain was moaning. I thought at first it might be the man with the fucked up leg, but this one was moaning about his arm. I got my phone out of the pocket of my discarded pants. The clock on the phone said it was 4:30 AM. I took a deep breath, then another one, and dialed the number. It rang five times before my frantic mother picked up. I started talking fast, explaining everything as quickly as possible before any kind of panic was able to set in. Panic comes from the unknown. It's better to get the unknown out of the way as quickly as possible. When I finished I could hear my mother breathing on the other side of the phone.

"Don't let them do any surgery until we get there."

"If they tell me they need to cut me open I'm not going to stop them."

"I'm going to call Uncle Tom."

"You don't need to do that."

"We're leaving here as soon as we can. I'd feel better if somebody was there."

"Mom…."

"I need to call Uncle Tom now. Call me back as soon as you know more."

The phone went dead. I lay back and stared up at the ceiling, feeling a little bored. My parents lived three hours away. My Uncle Tom was just over in Beaverton. Time passed. My moaning neighbor was wheeled out and a new groaning neighbor was moved in. The goo loving first sonogram guy pulled back the curtain. He wheeled me off to another dark room where a table moved me through a big plastic donut.

"Got any metal on ya?"

"Where the hell would I put it?"

The sonogram guy grunted, did his job, and wheeled me back to my alcove. My Uncle Tom was sitting in the chair. He looked tired and a little disgruntled, which is probably fair for that hour in the morning.

"How ya feeling?"

"I've been better. Sorry for having you come out."

"It's okay. I'm usually already up by now."

Such is the life of a thirty-one year old bachelor. A married man always has a wife ready to do the heavy lifting. Bachelors have random relatives chosen by proximity. Not that I thought my uncle held it against me, but I knew, even if I would never say it out loud, that if I was in his place I would feel a little put out. We both tried telling a joke or two, but they all fell flat. It was okay. Laughing, even polite half fake laughing, hurt quite a bit. The doctor came back in.

"Who's this?"

"My uncle."

"Is it okay to speak in front of him?"

"He's here ain't he?"

The doctor paused, his lips pursed.

"You have appendicitis."

"Okay."

"We're going to have to perform surgery to remove it."

"When?"

"We haven't figured that out yet. We'll be moving you up to the ICU."

The doctor left. My uncle leaned in.

"Think he smokes?"

I laughed, but cut it short. The nurse came in, put a tube in my arm, my clothes in a mesh bag, and unceremoniously wheeled me upstairs to the ICU. I didn't see the lobby nurse, which is too bad, I wanted her to see that there was actually something wrong with me.

I won't bore you with a lot of the following details, mostly because most of them are kind of cloudy. It was at this point, thanks to the presence of my uncle, that they gave me the good stuff. Suffice to say, I understood for the first time how people can get addicted to painkillers. It was a warm internal hug that spread from my arm across my body. The pain went away as though killed by the flip of a switch. I called my mother to let her know they were going to cut me open. Nobody answered so I tried her cell. Nobody answered again. Lots of dead zones between here and there. I left a message. We watched the sun rise. The floor nurse came through to check on me. She was an attractive younger woman with nice blue eyes and a big smile. When she left my uncle grinned.

"I think she liked you."

I didn't really know what to say. I really wasn't in any shape to take advantage of the situation even if she did. My mother called from her cell. I tried to talk to her for a bit, but my brain wasn't quite up to snuff, so I let my uncle talk to her instead. We watched a bit of early morning television and I took a nap. When I woke up my parents were there. They thanked my uncle, talked with him a bit, and sent him home. My mother was of course worried, the way mothers always are, though I got the sense she was enjoying the exercising of the motherly duties she could no longer provide for her two married sons. My father, looking tired, found a chair and sat down to wait. I was glad that my mother was there, though it meant that I would have to adapt my television watching to avoid anything too risqué, which luckily wasn't that hard to do at eight in the morning.

The surgery was scheduled for that evening. We mostly sat in the room and did nothing, me falling asleep from time to time and the nurse, a different one, coming in to do routine checks and pump me full of more painkillers. I wasn't allowed to eat, you know, because of the upcoming surgery, but my friend Mallory brought my parents some teriyaki chicken. My mother kept apologizing as she ate, but I didn't really care. You could've probably beaten the crap out of me and I would have still been on cloud nine. Again, I can understand how people get addicted to such things. At one point my brother, his wife, and my four year old niece came in for a visit. They were in town for a doctor appointment. We talked some, but it was obvious that my niece was a little scared. Me slurring my speech and slightly drooling probably didn't help any. Late in the afternoon the surgeon came in to shake my hand and explain the procedure. My mother asked all sorts of questions, but I mostly just nodded my head.

They wheeled me down around six. My parents were left to wait in yet another ubiquitous waiting room. They shaved my belly and started pumping me full of medical grade knockout drops. I can remember cracking a few jokes and becoming very worried that I would say something racist. I should have probably mentioned that the surgeon was black, though it really wasn't important until this moment. I'm not sure why I was worried about saying something racist. I've never really been the type to say racist things and none of my opinions were really all that racist beyond my own implicit biases, but for whatever reason while going under it was all I could think about. Either way, it would've been a hell of a time to become a racist, you know, right before someone starts slicing and dicing.

They cut me open around eight in the evening. It was one hell of a way to spend New Year's Eve. I don't remember any of it, because they put me out of course, but I was told that they pulled it out of a small hole they cut in my belly button. There were two other holes as well, one to the right and one below, where they shoved in other instruments. Apparently, they didn't bother to tell my parents when the surgery was done, just wheeled me back up to my room and left me without a word. My parents figured out that I was probably out of surgery when the janitor turned out the lights in the room they were in. I don't know. I was still asleep at that time.

When I woke up the next morning pretty much all my pain was gone. Even with the good stuff, though it didn't hurt, I could still feel that something was not quite right, that something was swelled up and pushing everything else out of the way. Yet another nurse took my vitals, this one cuter than the last, though not as cute as the first. The three holes in my belly looked as though they had been closed with hot glue. I was glad that they were letting me eat again, but a little disappointed that nobody had thought to ask whether or not I would be able to keep my recently removed organ. You can ask for a part they take out of your car, so why shouldn't you be able to ask for a part they took out of you? However, it was a little late by the time I thought of it. They kept me in the hospital for another day and a half, waiting for me to prove to them that I could poop, which is an interesting task when you're also ordered not to strain in any way. I finally managed to prove it, after which they cut me loose, though I was forced to take a complimentary wheelchair ride to the door.

After showing my father where my car was, which took a good twenty minutes of searching and backtracking, my mother took me home and helped me get into bed. My father left later that day, but my mother stayed for a couple more. I spent most of that time sleeping, while my mother cleaned my house and made a list of things I would need to buy to keep my house at the level of cleanliness she had brought it to. She left soon after, though only after repeated insistence that I would be fine. I'm pretty sure she only left because my friend Mallory declared that she was willing to take care of me. Five days after surgery, still confined mostly to my house, several of my friends came over to visit and keep me company. Nikki was wearing brand new glasses. Thank god. I'd hate to have thought of her running anybody over.

They Should've Told You At The Door

The Devil

The knock on the door came about 3:30 or so. I was sitting by the window, trying to keep cool, watching the cars drive by and doing a crossword puzzle. You know, usual lazy Saturday afternoon shit. It wasn't a hard knock. No, it was one of those light taps. The kind that makes you think the person on the other side might be a little shy or something. I don't think anything about it, so I put down my newspaper and glass of sun tea and walk over to the door. Now of course we don't have any peepholes, fucking peepholes are a luxury, so I just pull the door open to look and see who it is. I don't do any of that half open crap. I just pull it full open. You know me, what the hell do I have to worry about? Anyways, I pull the door open and there he is, the devil, just standing in the hall.

I know what you're thinking. How the hell did I know he was the devil? Ain't the devil supposed to be sneaky or something? I don't know much about that, but he was definitely the devil. Red skin, black goatee, cloven hooves, horns on his head. It was pretty hard to mistake him for anybody else. We just kind of sat there staring at each other for a while, him just kind of fidgeting in the hall, me just waiting for him to say something. I could tell he wanted something, and I really wanted him to make the first move, but I'm not the most patient man, especially when I have a glass of sun tea and crossword puzzle waiting for me.

Tiring of such crap, I finally said, "what you want devil?"

The devil took in a big breath and let it out. "It sure is hot out today," he said.

Ain't that something, the damn devil complaining about the heat. I shot right back, "can't be any hotter than hell I bet."

"We usually keep it at 65 degrees Celsius or so," said the devil.

"Celsius," I replied, "what the hell is that in Fahrenheit?"

"I don't know," he said with another sigh. "I think it's more the humidity. It's more of a dry heat in hell."

After that we just stood there looking at each other again. The fucker wouldn't get around to whatever the hell he wanted, and I sure as hell didn't want to stand by the damn door all day. The ice shifted in my sun tea and we both turned to look at the glass by the open window.

"Is that sun tea?" asked the devil.

"Yeah," I answered.

"Do you think I could have a glass?" he asked.

Now there was no way in hell that I was going to let the devil in my house. My mother didn't raise a damn fool.

"This ain't no trick, is it?" I said.

"Naw," replied the devil, "I was just damning a guy down the hall. Apartment 4E. I just didn't expect it to be so hot in this building."

Now this sounded plausible, after all, you know Mr. Monroe, dried up old piece of shit. Plus it was pretty fucking hot out in the hallway. So I said, "yeah, it is pretty fucking hot."

"You should get some air conditioning in this place," said the devil.

"Yeah," I replied, "that would be nice, but the landlord is a tight ass."

"Yeah," said the devil, "I believe that." Then he gave kind of a knowing chuckle like he knew the landlord or something. I don't know, my mother didn't raise no damn fool, but she didn't raise a rude bastard either. I mean shit, the guy might be the devil, but that was no reason to be impolite.

"If you wait here," I said, "I'll go get you a glass of sun tea."

"Thank you," answered the devil, "much obliged."

Well, I'm a fucking idiot. I went to the kitchen and poured the devil a big glass of sun tea, even wrapped it in a wet paper towel to keep it cool. Of course when I came back he was already in the apartment, peering at my pictures on the wall, his frickin hooves scuffing up the hardwoods. I should have known better, but I hadn't shut the door behind me, so now I had the devil in my home.

"I thought I told you to wait in the hall," I said.

"Sorry," said the devil, "it was just so hot out there. Just let me have my drink and I'll be going."

"Okay," I said, "just don't touch nothing."

There wasn't really much I could do. The devil was a big fella. You could tell that he worked out. He carried his arms the way weightlifters do, slightly out and bent at the elbows like he couldn't get them all the way down to his sides. It didn't really seem necessary to carry his arms like that, he wasn't the most cut guy I'd ever seen, but I was still pretty sure I couldn't shift him. The bastard noticed me looking at him and gave his arms a little flex.

"I can bench 285," he said.

"Ain't that something," I said.

I handed the devil his tea and he got himself settled on the couch. Swear to god it must have taken him five minutes. He kept adjusting the cushions and slightly changing his position. Those poor old couch springs were squeaking like a bag of mice.

Not knowing what else to do, I took back my position in the chair next to the window. The devil finally got himself settled, took a long sip of tea, and let out a sigh that sounded like it ought to have been coming from a lion.

"That's some good tea," he said.

"Thank you," I replied, "my mother taught me how to make some damn good sun tea."

"Would you mind watching your language," he said.

"Sorry," I answered.

We kind of sat there quiet for a while, him sipping his tea and playing with the edge of the paper towel, me staring out the window and doing my best to ignore him. Every now and again he'd say something, some crap about the weather or other such nonsense, you know, trying to start a conversation, but I'd only give him grunts in response. The devil was taking his sweet ass time with that sun tea. Just little sips every now and again, sometimes crunching on a chunk of ice. We probably sat there for an hour like that. Finally the last drops went in him and I started to perk up a bit. The devil didn't get up though, he just sat there on the couch, smacking his lips appreciatively.

"May I have another?" he asked.

"You said you just wanted one," I replied.

"I'm still pretty thirsty," he said.

Well now my blood was boiling, but what the hell was I supposed to do about it? The devil just sat there, blinking at me like an innocent lamb, his big red hands wrapped around the glass.

"Just one more glass," he said, "then I'll be going. Still a bit of damning to do today."

I said a few choice words under my breath, quiet enough where the devil wouldn't be able to make them out, but loud enough so he would know that I was doing it, got up, took his glass, and went back into the kitchen. I poured him another glass of sun tea from the pitcher and wrapped it with a fresh wet paper towel to keep it cool. When I went back into the main room the devil was still sitting on the couch, but he was looking at all my stuff. I didn't like how he was doing it. He was doing it in that way where you know someone thinks you decorate with tacky garbage, but they're not going to say anything because it would be impolite. I walked over and handed the devil back his glass.

"This is a nice place," he said, "what's it cost you in rent?"

"That's none of your business," I replied.

"Ever think about having a roommate?" he asked.

That was it for me. I could see where this was going from a mile away. "Don't need one," I said. "I prefer living alone."

"Really," said the devil, "I think I'd get lonely."

"Excuse me," I said, slipping back to the bedroom. I closed the door behind me, grabbed my phone from where it was charging on the bedside table, and went into the closet to make a call. You know how small my apartment is, and I sure the hell didn't want the devil to hear me. Things were getting out of hand and I needed help. Luckily, I knew a guy.

The phone rang six times before he picked up. "Hello," said Jesus. His voice sounded kind of loopy, like I just woke him up from a nap or something. I could hear a woman's voice in the background.

"Hello Jesus," I said, "It's Joe. I kind of got a bit of a problem."

"Jesus," said Jesus. "It's my day off."

"Sorry," I said, "but the devil's in my apartment and he won't get out."

"How'd he get in your apartment?" asked Jesus.

"He wanted some sun tea," I replied, "when I went to get it for him he just walked in."

"Ha," said Jesus, "classic devil."

"So you going to come over?" I asked.

"Christ Joe," he replied, "it's my one day off, and I probably shouldn't be driving."

"I go to church every Sunday Jesus," I said, "doesn't that count for anything anymore?"

"Fine," he said. "I'll be over in about fifteen minutes."

Jesus hung up on his end. I got out of the closet, plugged my phone back in, and went back into the main room. The devil was still sipping on his sun tea, though now he had his hooves up on my coffee table and was reading a People magazine through a pair of delicate reading glasses perched on his nose. I don't know where the hell he got it. I don't read People.

"Who were you talking to?" asked the devil.

"My mother," I replied.

The devil grinned in a way that made me want to punch him in the face. "How is she doing?" he asked.

"Fine," I said.

It took Jesus forty-five minutes to get to my apartment. Forty-five minutes of watching the devil sip sun tea and make snarky remarks about celebrities. The knock on the door was forceful, several quick hard raps.

The devil glanced over his reading glasses. "Who could that be?" he asked.

"I'll go see," I replied.

Jesus was a little worse for wear. When I answered the door he was wearing a stained AC-DC t-shirt and a pair of baggy Bermuda shorts that made his thin white legs look like toothpicks. His shaggy hair was pulled back in a ponytail and his beard was pretty ratty. He smelled a little bit. Grumpy is the term I'd use to describe his face. After a perfunctory greeting Jesus pushed past me into the main room. His eyes tracked across my stuff.

"Christ what a bunch of crap," he said.

The devil was eying Jesus from the couch. "What are you doing here?" he asked.

48

Jesus clapped his hands together and gestured towards the door. "Time to leave man. Let's go."

The devil casually took off his reading glasses and returned them to a case in his pocket. "I thought today was your day off," he said.

Jesus chewed on the insides of his cheeks and narrowed his eyes. He was shivering with impatience. "Lucifer Beelzebub Satan," he said, "it's time to get your ass out of here."

"No," answered the devil, "I kind of like it here. It's very homey, plus I haven't finished my magazine yet."

Jesus was really pissed. You should have seen him. Just shaking. "C'mon man," he said, "I got a girl down from Seattle. She's got to catch the train tomorrow. I don't have time for this shit."

"Not my problem," replied the devil.

"Damn it," said Jesus.

"Watch your language," said the devil.

"Fuck it," said Jesus, and with that he charged forward and tried to manhandle the devil off the couch. It went exactly as well as you can imagine. Jesus probably didn't weigh 130 pounds soaking wet. The devil let Jesus pull and twist at him for about a minute, and then, growing tired of it, casually threw Jesus to the floor with the indifference of a man throwing away a used tissue. I scrambled forward to help Jesus up, because you know, he's Jesus.

"Are you alright?" I asked.

"Do you have a phone?" he questioned.

"Yeah," I said, "in the bedroom."

"Be right back," he said, and with that Jesus went into my bedroom and shut the door behind him. The devil got back out his reading glasses and went back to his People magazine. I sat back down by the window and clenched my fists. The devil peered at me over the top of his glasses.

"You know," he said, "letting yourself get so stressed out is going to take years off your life." I didn't answer. Jesus came out of the bedroom. "Who did you call," asked the devil, "your dad?"

"No," said Jesus, sitting down on the other side of the couch. "Whatever," said the devil.

"Can I have some sun tea?" asked Jesus.

"Me too," said the devil, rattling the ice in his empty glass.

What else could I do? I mean after all, the guy did come all the way over to try and help me, even if it wasn't working out so well. So I went in the kitchen and fixed them both up a glass of sun tea, pouring out the last of the pitcher. When I came back into the main room the devil was making comments about celebrities again, while Jesus mostly chewed on his fingernails and kept glancing at the apartment door. Things stayed that way for probably around half an hour before someone knocked. I started to rise, but Jesus beat me to the jump, springing up and rushing to the door like an anxious girl waiting for her prom date. The devil and I sat waiting, listening to muffled voices before Jesus came back into the main room, followed by a tall man in a blue uniform.

"Really," said the devil, "you called the police."

Jesus pointed at the devil with an imperious finger. "That's him officer. That's the trespasser."

The policeman pushed his way past Jesus, his face stern until the moment he got a good look at the culprit. The devil smiled oh so sweet and the officer grinned in return.

"Lucifer, you old so and so", said the officer, "how are you?"

"Doing well Frank," replied the devil, "how's the kids?"

"Fine, just fine," said the officer, "growing like weeds. You going to make Roy's barbecue next week?"

"I was planning to," said the devil.

This was all a bit too much for Jesus I'm afraid. He stood there, mouth agape, sucking air, and finally managed to squeeze out a single bark of an expletive.

"Fuck," said Jesus.

"Is there any problem here Luci?" asked the police officer.

"No," said the devil, "just a bit of a misunderstanding."

"Alright then," said the police officer.

Jesus kept looking from the devil, to the police officer, to me. Tears of frustration were flowing down his cheeks. I just felt numb, though I did feel pretty sorry for Jesus. It had to be pretty embarrassing having a breakdown like that in front of everybody. With his face bright red, he fled out into the hall. The devil blew air out through his lips with exasperation and then gestured towards me.

"Do we have any more sun tea?"

"No," I replied. "We're all out."

"That's a shame," said the devil, turning to the police officer. "I'm sorry Frank, afraid we can't be as hospitable as I hoped."

"That's okay," said the police officer. "Is that fella going to be alright?"

"Don't worry about him," replied the devil. "Sometimes he just gets that way."

So that was that. That's the whole story. I can tell you think it's a bunch of bullshit, but it's the honest truth. Do you understand now? That's why I stole your hundred dollars and slept with your fine ass cousin, because the devil's in my apartment. I have the devil living with me and there isn't a damn thing I can do about it.

They Should've Told You At The Door

Chocolates

When I was a young boy the small town I grew up in didn't have the Boy Scouts or Girl Scouts, but for one year it did have Campfire, which was basically Scouts Lite where you had to wear a dorky vest. As part of the Campfire experience, we were given boxes of chocolates to sell door to door to raise money for some reason.

Now it must be understood that I've always had a bit of a sweet tooth. I know lots of people think they have a sweet tooth, but my case was pretty severe, probably more comparable to a crack addiction than a sweet tooth if we're being honest. Whenever my parents left me home alone, I would eat two or three cups of straight sugar and then run around the house like an idiot whacked out on the sweet taste of cane. During one of these sucrotic trips I actually ran into a wall so hard that I knocked myself out. Luckily, I woke up before my parents got home and cleaned up the blood so they were none the wiser.

Anyways, given the above, it goes without saying that I of course hid in my room and started eating Campfire chocolates pretty much as soon as I got them home. It was a rush. They had four different types and I gorged myself on all but one. That one being coconut which is just gross. By the time everything was all said and done I polished off somewhere in the vicinity of twenty boxes of chocolates. It would have been more, but again, I didn't like coconut and that was all I had left.

Coming down off of my high, I realized that twenty ill-gotten boxes of chocolates left a lot of evidence. Throwing them in the garbage was not really an option given the sheer amount of evidence, so instead I came up with the clever idea of hiding them in my dresser until I could figure out what the hell I was going to do. That night I slept with a lot of guilt, but luckily, I did not have to live with it long given that my Mom pretty quickly noticed that my dresser was full of garbage when I got dressed the next morning.

Well, the truth came out pretty quickly because while the powers to be might have given the younger version of me a propensity for lying they sure as hell didn't make me any good at it. In the end, after the usual series of lectures, my parents paid for the chocolates and made me work to pay them back. At the next Campfire meeting I got a special congratulations for selling my chocolates so quickly.

When I think back on this story, I still feel a lot of guilt for what I did, but just between you and me, I also feel a strange sense of pride for eating twenty boxes of chocolates in a single sitting.

Centaur

"You know," Gary said, "it's not easy being a centaur."

I lowered my eyes to the tabletop and took a long sip of coffee, hoping that Gary would catch the hint that I didn't really want to talk about it, but of course, as always, he missed my cues.

"Some people think it must all just be great, but I'll tell you what, it's not great at all."

We were sitting in Kalo Kafe, a coffee place just off 48th. Okay, I was sitting. Gary was more laying, his long muscular legs tucked beneath him, his head just a little lower than mine. Kalo Kafe was far from the best coffee place in town. In truth their coffee always tasted burnt, but it was roomy enough to accommodate Gary's size.

"Just look at getting here," said Gary, the words punctuated with a sharp cut of his hand towards the street. "It's not like I can just ride a bus or take a taxi. I had to walk some eighty blocks just to have a coffee."

Gary wasn't drinking coffee. He was drinking a hot chocolate with extra whipped cream, a portion of which dotted his goatee. I thought momentarily of bringing up this misstatement of fact but decided against it. There was little chance of it derailing Gary's rant. No, a defensive tone would probably be better.

"You were the one who chose this place," I said quietly right before taking another sip of my so-called Colombian blend.

Gary swelled his muscular chest at the challenge.

"I had to pick this place. Do you know how few coffee shops in this city are ready to handle a centaur? I tried a nice little place in my neighborhood just last week and they had to move half the tables out of the way just so I could sit down. The manager had to ask a couple to move seats. Do you have any idea how embarrassing it was?"

My eyes broke away and roved across the art on the coffee shop's walls. A dozen or so brightly colored drawings of celebrities both living and dead with hundreds of words in a thin precise hand scrawled over the top of everything. The price tags beneath each ranged from two hundred to seven hundred dollars with no discernible pattern based on size or complexity. With a sigh I returned to the conversation.

"Well, at least you're getting a lot of exercise."

"Exercise," scoffed Gary, "fucking exercise." His tail was twitching, and I silently prayed that it wouldn't start swishing through the air.

"I'm just saying I wish I could run over thirty miles per hour."

"Do you have any idea how hard all this pavement and concrete is on my hooves? I have to wear rubber booties. Do you know how much they cost? How quickly they wear out?"

"Why don't you just wear horseshoes?"

I knew the words were a mistake the moment they left my mouth. I wished desperately that I could suck them back in. Gary's face hung loosely from his skull, a sallow mix of anger, sadness, and disappointment. His tail gave a single agitated flick

56

which brushed the back of the woman at the next table. She turned around, saw Gary's twitching frame, and returned back to her own business.

"Horseshoes! Fucking horseshoes are for riding. Have you ever seen anybody riding me?"

I could feel that my face was flushed with embarrassment. My fingers nervously played with my napkin, my eyes studying their every movement.

"No."

"So would it make any sense for me to wear horseshoes?"

"No."

"See, this is what I'm talking about, just plain old fashion ignorance."

Gary pounded the table with a closed fist, rattling our cups on their saucers. My napkin was nothing but torn shreds of paper. I took a deep breath and let it out. It wasn't worth getting angry over.

"I'm sorry."

Gary's face softened. He could be a pitbull, but he always turned back into a puppy when someone showed him their belly.

"It's okay. I'm sorry for getting all riled up."

"No worries."

"It just all gets me so mad sometimes."

"No worries."

The woman from behind the counter walked up to our table, her mouth a hard straight line, her eyes just a little nervous.

"Is everything all right over here?"

Gary flashed his best smile. He was really quite handsome when he smiled.

"Yes, everything's just fine."

The straight course of the woman's mouth wavered a little.

"Things sounded like they were getting a little heated over here."

Gary's smile widened and he gave a flirtatious flick with his tail, hitting the woman at the next table again. She did her level best to ignore the intrusion.

"My apologies. Just a little political talk amongst friends."

The woman from behind the counter's hard exterior was melting before my very eyes.

"Okay then, just try to keep it down. You're not the only customers you know."

"Of course." Gary held out a giant hand. "I'm Gary by the way."

The woman took his hand, her small fingers completely disappearing within his.

"Chloe."

"Charmed."

Gary held on a little longer than what most people would've considered comfortable. Chloe didn't seem to mind. When they finally broke apart, she was visibly smiling.

"Okay, you boys let me know if you need anything else."

Gary winked so subtly I almost missed it.

"But of course."

Chloe walked back behind the counter. Gary's eyes watched her the whole way. I took a drink of coffee and set the cup down hard enough to draw his attention.

"She seemed nice."

Gary glanced towards her again.

"Very nice."

"You could probably get her number."

"I imagine so."

"Are you going to do it?"

Gary shifted himself into a more comfortable position and took a drink of cocoa.

"Probably not."

"Why the hell not?"

Gary put down his cup. It looked ridiculous in his big hands.

"What do you want me to do? Disembowel the poor girl?"

I choked on my drink of coffee. Gary watched silently, waiting for me to regain my composure. I set down my cup and coughed a few times. Gary casually scratched one of his front fetlocks before speaking.

"You see, this is exactly what I was talking about. Nobody knows how difficult it is to be a centaur."

I inwardly groaned. I had hoped that the topic was finished.

"I mean look at me. Really look at me. What do you see?"

I could barely control not rolling my eyes.

"A centaur Gary. I see a centaur."

"And what is a centaur?"

Gary's finger poked the table with every word.

"Christ Gary."

His finger poked the table again.

"And what is a centaur?"

"Half man and half horse."

Gary's thick digit raised victoriously into the air.

"Exactly. Half man and half fucking horse. So, which am I supposed to be attracted to? The woman or the mare?"

I slouched in my seat, feeling uncomfortable, my eyes and mind seeking any avenue of escape. A man on the other side of the cafe was sipping a cappuccino. I prayed for him to drop it.

"I don't know Gary."

Gary was too deep in to notice my discomfort. He surged forward with wild abandon.

"Sure, the mare would make the most sense from a physiological point of view, but she's still just a mare. A dumb animal. Is that what I must stoop too? Bestiality? And the woman. The poor woman. Sure, the conversations can be wonderful, but I don't think I have to say out loud the intimate limitations that ought to be obvious to both of us. Never mind the ones who just want to go out for the thrill of being seen on a date with a centaur. Can you imagine being treated as nothing more than a sideshow act for some freak's fancies?"

I was sick of it. It had been three months since last time I hung out with Gary, and it was quickly becoming apparent why so much time had been allowed to elapse. We had been friends for a long time, but there was really only so much a person can take. I surged upwards in my seat, back snapping straight, neck craning forward.

"Fuck Gary. Why don't you just date a centaur then?"

Gary surged back. His big hands gripped the table. One of his rubber encased hooves scraped along the tile with agitation.

"Oh sure, it's so easy for you. Do you think there's just some dating app for centaurs? When was the last time you even saw another centaur in this city?"

"I don't know Gary."

"There are none. It's just me. Just lonely old me."

"Then why don't you just move to a place with more centaurs?"

Gary was taken aback by such a suggestion.

"What, and just throw away my career? My friends? Everything?"

With every comeback I slunked lower in my chair. People were beginning to stare. The once happy face of Chloe was looking dour once again. There was only one hope for escape. One last desperate lunge at some kind of sanity.

"Can we change the subject please."

"I'm just saying…."

"Can we please just change the subject."

"I….."

"Gary, please."

Gary took a deep breath and let it out. He inhaled and exhaled again. His shoulders fell. His hands unclenched. His tail twitched nervously. His eyes turned downward with embarrassment.

"I'm sorry. I got a little carried away."

I reached over and patted his arm.

"It's okay Gary. It's okay. Let's just talk about something else."

Gary smiled weakly. The kind of smile that said I know I fucked up but thank you for being my friend. He gestured at me with his hand.

"How's your job going?"

"It's going pretty well. Might be up for a promotion soon."

A mother and child came into the cafe. The child was probably no older than five. He stared at Gary with great interest then tugged on his mother's skirt to get her attention. She bent over and he whispered something into her ear, one chubby arm pointing over at my friend. Gary was doing his level best to ignore them, politely nodding as I filled him in on the latest happenings at my work. The mother took the child by the hand and walked over to our table, courteously waiting for us to take notice of her. If it was me, I would've just ignored her, but Gary has never been able to deal with anything in a fashion other than head on. When he spoke, his voice was low and his face neutral.

"Can I help you?"

The woman motioned towards her progeny who was happily picking his nose.

"Hello," she said, voice as sweet as syrup. "Would it be okay if my son climbs on your back for a picture?"

"Excuse me?"

Gary's voice was full of menace. I could see every muscle on his body tense and could feel mine do the same. The woman must have been completely clueless. She pressed on with the same tone as before, smiling brightly down at us.

"Would it be okay if my son got on your back and I took a picture. He's never seen a centaur before."

"Fuck you."

The mother drew her spawn closer to her body, a protective arm wrapped in front of him.

"Well, a simple no would have sufficed. There's no need to curse in front of my son."

Gary was growing red in the face. He lifted himself ponderously. First his front half and then his back, his rubber encased feet slipping on the tiles with sharp squeaks. His voice rose with his body.

"Fuck you lady. Fuck you. Fuck you. Fuck you."

He was nearly yelling. I slouched down in my chair as low as I could. The mother took a step back, dragging her son with her.

"You're causing a scene."

It was true. Gary was causing a scene. Everyone in the cafe was staring at him. Chloe was starting to work her way around the counter, her face grim. Gary's tail whipped with agitation, catching the woman at the table behind him across the side of the face. Her balled fists pounded the table and she rose, her voice nearly shrill.

"Will you please quick hitting me with your god damn tail."

Gary turned to look at the woman, his haunches grazing the wall, knocking one of the garishly colored celebrity drawings to the floor.

"Fuck you too."

Chloe dove into the middle of everything, interposing herself between Gary and the leering eyes of the spectators.

"I'm going to have to ask you to go."

Gary's breathing was ragged. One back hoof pawed the ground. He looked at Chloe, then at the mother and son, and then down at me doing my best to turn invisible. His eyes tracked across the faces of the crowd, searching for any sign of an ally. The best that was there was neutral curiosity. He pointed at the masses.

"Fuck all of you."

Chloe gestured towards the door.

"Out."

Gary took a few breaths to regain his composure and nodded.

"My apologies. I'll be on my way."

He moved towards the door. The mother whispered loudly to the woman at the next table.

"He's more beast than man."

Gary's hind leg shot out in a blur, catching a small table on the rim. The table tipped and slammed against the wall, coffee cups smashing on the floor, chairs falling as the table's two occupants rushed to get out of the way. Chloe was about to yell something, but Gary was already gone, yanking the door shut behind him. The crowd began murmuring. The little boy pointed out the big front window.

"Look Momma, he's pooping on the sidewalk."

People crowded forward to see. I stared at the table in front of me, down at Gary's cup still a quarter full of hot chocolate. My voice was soft, so quiet that I doubt anyone else could hear the words drop from my lips.

"He doesn't fit in the toilets."

They Should've Told You At The Door

Overlook

I stopped at the overlook because I was tired. My bad knee had left in me far from the best of shape, and the heat drained whatever else I had left in me. Aside from the boiling weather it was a nice evening, punctuated by the buzz of a few bugs floating in the air and the chug of the trains in the yard below. Across the river the sun was starting to set down into the hills covered by the lights of far off porches just starting to fade from the world. It felt nice at the overlook. It always felt nice.

She was standing beneath the apple tree, surrounded by the sweet smell of the ripening fruit. She was young, maybe early twenties, maybe not even out of high school. It's harder to tell the older that you get. She was wearing high waisted shorts that hugged her ass, and a crop top without a bra underneath. Her apparel left no secrets. You could see everything. Long dark hair cascaded down her back. She had the tight diminutive shape of her age and those big innocent eyes that set some men on fire and cause others to shudder with dread. She was looking out at the lights on the hills across the river, one hand holding a phone to her ear, and the other supporting her arm as though the weight of it was too great to bear.

I kept my distance. No need to cause a stir by standing too close. There was plenty of view from where I stood. Though I kept well away I could hear her voice floating on the breeze. It was no more than a harsh whisper, but it found its way to me all the same.

"Billy. I can you see Billy. I'm looking at your house right now."

It was a husky voice, raw as though she had spent the whole day screaming, with every syllable sharper than a tack. I found myself standing perfectly still, holding my breath, nothing but the beating of my heart to interrupt. I leaned in. Oh lord I leaned in. I'll admit it, but I challenge any to claim they wouldn't have done the same.

"I can smell you Billy. I can smell you all over me. Your scent is driving me wild Billy. It's making me so wet."

She took in a ragged breath and let it out, shaking her entire exterior. Her loose breasts beneath her shirt heaved their way upward and fell. A shiver coursed through her entire body. I trembled. God save me, but I trembled. I could feel the primal heat. Her head remained locked in place, unaware of the world around her beyond some far off light that marked some boy on the other side.

"Do you remember what I told you Billy? Do you remember? You better not be cranking it Billy. You better not be turning that knob. They're mine Billy. Every single one belongs to me. You remember that Billy. You remember what I said. You wait Billy. You wait, or god knows what I'll do."

She must have been leaving a voicemail, for she never gave any chance to answer. She hung up her phone and held it close to her heart. She stared out across the river with a gaze more intense than an old hound with a raccoon up a tree. I was still tired, but I decided to move on. God thank you for the smarts to know when it's time to move on.

They Should've Told You At The Door

Siskiyou

On October 14, at 2:00 PM, while most people were at work, one of Oregon's U.S. Senators hosted a public meeting in Ashland, Oregon to allow the Department of the Interior to hear comments and gauge support for a proposed doubling in size of the Siskiyou National Monument. The activists were ready. The officials from the Department of the Interior were greeted by a sea of supporters, wearing matching t-shirts and waving professionally made signs. Others weren't ready, notably the area's rural communities, ranchers, loggers, and Bureau of Land Management offices. Some didn't get notice until late Friday on October 7, well after normal closing hours, others didn't get any notification at all, having to hear about it through the grapevine. Not only were they poorly informed about the meeting, but it was also the first they had ever heard that their senator was making such a proposal on their behalf, a proposal the Senator claimed, in a letter dated August 25, had broad local support. Opponents gathered as many people as they could, but by meeting time, the difference in preparation was obvious. Unfortunately, things like this are fairly common.

In rural Oregon, conservation groups, especially the larger ones, tend to swing pretty big hammers. With budgets that surpass many of the rural economies they work in (thanks to large donations from urban areas, with much coming from out of state), they are able to afford full time lawyers and activists, political connections, and the high cost of organizing people and events; costs which are far beyond the means of the opposing ranchers and other groups (both in terms of funds, time available, and people available). While in our minds we like to view the plucky environmentalists, with a shoestring budget, fighting against the evil corporations and their millions of dollars, in rural Oregon the reality is often the opposite.

This doesn't mean that conservation is a bad thing, in fact, you'd be hard pressed to find anyone in rural Oregon who doesn't support conservation, but only if it's the kind of conservation that's based on science and compromise. Not the kind that's based on a fanaticism that borders on religious zealotry, and certainly not the kind that depends on near constant lawsuits, backroom dealings, and intimidation.

Regardless of whatever side you have on an issue, it's important to empathize and try to understand the other side. So, look at it from rural Oregon's perspective. Take a look through their eyes at what they consider thirty plus years of broken government promises. Thirty plus years of taking the full economic cost of conservation decisions made by people hundreds or thousands of miles away. Thirty plus years of watching their economies shrink, unemployment rates rise, and dependency on government welfare grow. Thirty plus years of watching the biggest employer become the government. Thirty plus years of being told that their only hope is to try and become a tourist spot, hoping that their area is comparatively pretty enough for urbanites to come out and take a look. Thirty plus years of being on the political sidelines, feeling they aren't represented. Thirty plus years of facing down million dollar groups who see them not as people, but only as obstacles to an agenda or goal. Thirty plus years of being made villains by people who have never talked to them and have never tried to understand them or their issues. Thirty plus years of being called hicks and rednecks, of being assumed to be ignorant simply because of where they live. Thirty plus years of being told their problems don't matter because some other group has had it worse. Thirty plus years of feeling pushed around.

Here in Portland, we cheer on protesters who call out against rising home prices and rental rates, police contracts, banks and big business, and even far off pipelines in North Dakota. Even in cases where we ourselves do not feel the need to protest, we can at least understand where the protesters are coming from. In all these cases people are feeling that their voices are no longer being heard. In all these cases people feel like the political system is failing them, that they don't have a place at the table, that they're getting ground up by a machine fueled by who has the most money and lawyers. In all these cases, people are increasingly feeling like they have no other options. Well, agree with them or not, that's how many people in rural Oregon feel.

The recent Bundy/Malheur verdict angered a lot of people I know. For me it's less concrete. I don't support Bundy and his brand of nutjobs. I don't support their tactics, and I certainly don't subscribe to their belief system. Yet, part of me has to cheer, because for the first time in my life, I saw issues that have been affecting the world I grew up in, issues normally kept to at best rural newspapers, talked about on the national news. Here's the thing, within every group of people, there is a group like the Bundy's. The kind of people, when things get bad, go off on some wacko tangent that has little to do with the actual problem, and do something crazy and idiotic. These people rarely represent a group as a whole, and it's easy to write them off as just a bunch of wackos, but it doesn't mean that there aren't some very legitimate problems that really need to be looked at.

In the end what you do with your time and your money is your business. All I'd ask is when issues like this come up, try to picture it through the eyes of the other side. Do they have a place at the table? Do they have a chance to speak? Are their views being treated in a respectful manner? We can work together to make a better world, a world of compromise and reason, but only if everyone has a voice.

Date Play By Play

Recently I started online dating again, which luck would have it, led to an actual in real life date this very night. Here is how the date went down:

1) On my way to the date a group of bros in a car with Arkansas plates decide to try and hit my car. I respond by of course flipping them the bird, which results in them swerving halfway into my lane again while yelling the N word at me. This of course puts me in the perfect mood to meet somebody for the first time.

2) My date texts me to let me know she will be late. I use this half hour to enjoy the nice weather on the patio and drink an entire beer, thus guaranteeing I'll be in the perfect mental state for a first date with a stranger.

3) My date arrives. I order my second beer and she orders her first. She starts things off by stating that first dates are pretty much job interviews and then launches into a fairly intense line

of questioning with me doing my failing best to get the same information from her.

4) Perhaps I shouldn't have mentioned that I'm unemployed. From now on I think I'm just going to say I'm on sabbatical or independently wealthy, which is technically true at least for the next few months.

5) Apparently this woman dislikes all of my hobbies.

6) Cleverly switching gears, I get her talking about her own life and hobbies. Hooray. Listening is easier than talking.

7) Good god is she really into horseback riding. I finish my beer and think about getting another even though she hasn't even finished her first one.

8) At this point a bird shits on my head and shoulder. It's about a dollop of shit. How much is a dollop you ask? Slightly more than you're imagining.

9) The bathroom door is locked, forcing me to stand in the crowded bar with a bird turd on my head and shoulder for a period of time that undoubtedly feels longer than it actually is.

10) I forget to lock the bathroom door, resulting in a ten year old boy opening it to reveal me with my shirt off to the world. Best case scenario, everyone now thinks I'm one of those weirdos who takes off their shirt to use the bathroom. Worst case, oh great, another public restroom pervert.

11) I buy another beer. I've earned it. There's a man dressed as a monk at the bar, or perhaps he's an actual monk. I chat with him while I wait for my beer. I seriously consider abandoning

my date to continue conversing with him about his favorite distilleries around town.

12) Lots of awkward jokes and comments about the fact that a bird fucking shit on me. I decide to try and lighten the mood with an off color joke on a different topic.

13) Awkward silence.

14) I get her talking about horses again.

15) I finish my third beer. She says she needs to get home and go to bed even though it's only eight o'clock. She leaves to close out her card. Instead of doing it at the same time, I awkwardly wait until she's done and then go to the bar to close out my own card.

16) I say good night and flee. I eat Thai food on my way home.

They Should've Told You At The Door

The Dance

"Hey little brother, we're going to the dance."

Dusty could hear the slur in Toby's voice, even over the phone. By the sound of it his brother was at least a half rack in.

"I thought you said nobody wanted to go."

"Tweeter's had a day. We need to get him out of the house."

"You said the dance was going to be gay."

There was a pause on the other end.

"Well, guess I'll just have to kiss a man then."

Toby laughed.

"We're going to pick you up in twenty minutes. Be ready."

The phone hung up. Dusty put down his cell and groaned. *Cannonball Run* was paused on the TV. The clock on the wall said 8:15. He could just hit play and pretend the call never happened. No, they'd just come in after him then. Besides, it might be fun. Do a little drinking. Do a little dancing. Maybe find a nice gal for a little something something. Dusty hit stop, got up with a groan, and went to find his pants. He considered for a moment grabbing a clean pair and a western shirt but decided not to. Fuck it. The jeans he'd been wearing all week and a t-shirt would be good enough. Get dressed. Brush his teeth. Comb his hair. Put on a ballcap. He thought about putting a dab of Stetson cologne on but settled with spraying his pants with Green Apple Glade air freshener. The dance was up at the Ag Pavilion. It probably wasn't going to be worth too much effort. It took Dusty about fifteen minutes to get ready. Toby knocked on the door at 9:00. His moonface, just like Dusty's but rounder, was split by a shit eating chew splattered grin.

Dusty thought about grabbing a coat but didn't. It was still pretty warm for early October. Joe was driving his extended cab pickup. Dusty was glad to see it. He was the Freshman. The back seat might be cramped, but it was a hell of a lot better than riding in the bed. Toby handed Dusty a Hamms from a case on the floorboards and pulled back the seat to let him in. The front seat creaked when Toby got in. He was a big boy. Joe, all knees and elbows, had a beer between his skinny legs. Tweeter was riding bitch. He looked pretty bad. The whole right side of his face was covered in red pin pricks with a couple of bigger gashes here and there. Dusty opened his beer and gestured towards Tweeter.

"What happened to him?"

Tweeter's eyes were half glazed over. He mumbled something, laughed, and then took a sloppy drink from his beer, spilling a bit down his chin. Toby laughed and even Joe managed a grin. He put the pickup in gear and cocked his head to the side to answer.

"Professor Tweeter is the victim of a failed science experiment."

Dusty looked at his older brother who's Cheshire grin was ringed by several days' worth of unshaved stubble. Toby gestured with his beer.

"One of the gallon wine jugs we put the beer into blew up. Must not have been as done brewing as we thought."

Joe drove the pickup up to the top of the hill and out of the trailer park, turning towards the bright lights of campus down the other side.

"I told you guys just to throw what was left out once you ran out of bottles."

Toby shrugged.

"Hated to waste it. I guess now we know. Who would of thought the screw top on a Carlo Rossi jug would be tougher than the glass."

Tweeter pounded the dash with one hand.

"I was just doing homework. Boom. Glass everywhere."

Toby laughed.

"That's right buddy."

Joe looked annoyed about the pounding on the dash.

"Christ, what do you expect putting all those dregs in there. Shit's full of yeast."

Toby shrugged.

"We thought it would settle out."

Toby laughed again. Dusty laughed with him. Toby's laugh was a little infectious. Tweeter tried to laugh too, but it only came out as a hissing wheeze. The road around the Ag Pavilion was crowded with cars and trucks, part of each halfway in the ditch. Joe pulled down by a group of tractors next to a building covered in sheet metal. He turned off the truck and gestured towards the case.

"Pass me another one sir."

Toby popped the top and passed it over.

"Gladly."

Dusty leaned forward from the back.

"Frank and Grandma going to care if you park down here?"

Joe gave Dusty a look that suggested Dusty was a little mentally deficient. Joe was only a Sophomore. Dusty hated that look.

"Do those old bastards work in the evening?"

"No."

"Then I probably wouldn't worry about it."

Toby passed Dusty back another beer. Dusty sucked the rest of his down and passed back up his empty. Joe hated finding empties in his truck, unless he or Toby were the ones who put them there. Toby was a Senior. Age had its privileges. Tweeter was a Senior too, or at least he would be if he went to half his classes. The four sat in the truck until 10:00. Dusty kept quiet, just glad to be included. He knew they wouldn't go in until the case was done. As the beer started to run out, Joe pulled out a flask and passed it around, even to Dusty. It was tequila. It made Dusty cough a bit when he sucked it down which made Toby laugh. It didn't matter. Dusty was starting to feel relaxed. Joe put in a CD and they sang a couple Jason Boland songs. Toby finished off the last beer. They headed to the dance, all except Tweeter, who they left sleeping in the truck.

The Ag Pavilion wasn't used for much beyond state FFA contests, and those only happened once a year. The whole place smelled of cobwebs and musty wood. The sawdust that normally covered the floor had been mostly scooped away by a Bobcat to one end behind the DJ. A Collegiate FFA girl took five bucks from each of them at the door. Dusty paid for Toby in return for the beer he drank. He was feeling a little light on his feet. Once they got inside, he went off to mingle with the crowd. There were a couple of girls he knew so he asked each of them to dance, twirling them within the mass of country swing moves on the dance floor still half covered with sawdust. It was an eclectic crowd. Everything from country shirts and cowboy hats, to ballcaps and t-shirts, to guys in polos with studs in their ears. Most of the girls wore open western shirts over tank tops. No matter the background, most of them seemed to have a better idea of what someone was supposed to wear to such things.

Dusty was having a hell of a time. Go dancing with a girl. Shoot the shit with a couple of guys he knew from class. Go out dancing again. Sometimes he'd run into his brother or Joe in the crowd and they'd offer him a drink from a flask. Tequila from Joe and whiskey from Toby. Dusty wondered how many flasks the two had on them. The world was a whirling mess that went straight to his head. Thin ones. Fat ones. In between ones. Big boobs. Little boobs. Dusty danced with all of them, yelling at them so his jokes would make it to their ears. One bigger girl kept a hold of him after a song and drug him off towards a corner for a kiss or two, Dusty's hands scrabbling along her muffin top, knocking ajar the extra tampon she had shoved in the band of her jeans at the small of her back. It fell to the ground. The girl yelped with embarrassment and Dusty laughed. Red in the face she ran off. Dusty wandered across the dance floor to find the bathroom.

The bathroom wasn't big. Three urinals and a shitter with no stall door. Some guy was washing his hands and three others, all in polo shirts, were drinking beers they must have smuggled in while one of their number went on about something he was apparently upset about. Dusty didn't bother to listen. With a slight lilt in his step he maneuvered his way to a urinal and let loose. With a belch he jiggled it off and put his dick away. The guy washing his hands was gone. One of the three polo shirts gestured at him.

"Hey, you want a beer?"

Dusty lunged back in overdone surprise.

"Sure, don't mind if I do."

The guy pulled out a Busch Light and handed it over. It joined its fellows already in Dusty's belly without issue. The one polo shirt guy, the one with studs in his ear, was still going on about something. He was obviously mad. Red in the face. The other two kept nodding. Dusty was having a bit of a hard time focusing. The generous member of the group nudged Dusty with his elbow.

"My buddy's pissed because some fucker keeps dancing with his girlfriend."

Dusty nodded in an exaggerated fashion.

"Well all right then."

"If shit goes down. You got our backs?"

Dusty squinted to try to get a better look at his three new compatriots. Nope. He definitely didn't know them, but then again, on the other hand, they had been nice enough to give him a beer. They were all three big guys. The kind of guys who spent a lot of time at the Rec Center. It seemed better to just kind of go along with it.

"Okay."

The generous one nodded. The angry one shouted something. The other two pounded his arms and yelled something back. They headed out the door. Dusty followed. The pack pushed its way towards the center of the dance floor, Dusty trailing in their wake. Their eyes were flashing across the crowd, searching for the promised adversary. The generous one was keeping close to Dusty, making sure he was still coming. With a sharp turn of his head, he gestured towards a couple dancing a two step near the DJ.

"There's the fucker."

Dusty's unsure gaze followed the pointed finger. The girl was in a white crop top over too tan skin, her blonde hair in ringlets. The guy was all knees and elbows but had a cocky grin and a cowboy hat tipped back on his head. It was Joe. The three behemoths in polo shirts started pushing their way through the crowd towards their target. Dusty hung back, unsure what to do. Some random potbellied guy in a collarless Garth Brooks shirt came ten stepping by with a girl in a side embrace. He bumped into Dusty. Dusty spun and punched the guy in the face. The girl screamed as her partner went down, blood pouring from his nose. The three polo shirts turned back to see what all the commotion was. Dusty yelled at them over the crowd.

"Wasn't this the guy?"

The generous one tried to yell back.

"No you stupid fucker. It was…."

The rest got lost in the commotion. Everybody in the damn place must have been the random guy's friend. A punch caught Dusty in the back of the head and he went down next to the poor son of a bitch who didn't deserve to get punched in the first place. The woman scored a few good kicks on Dusty's back before somebody pulled her away so they could take their turn. The polo shirts waded in, throwing themselves at the guy punching Dusty, just in time to catch the second wave of the random guy's friends coming in. Screams and yells drowned out the music. People were scattering to get out of the way while others crowded to get in closer. Dusty tried to get up, but somebody hit him in the back of the head again and he went back down. Somebody stepped on his hand. He covered his head and curled up into a ball. Big hands grabbed him and pulled him up. Dusty swung but didn't connect. The big hands started dragging him towards the door.

"Quit fighting you dumb shit."

Toby's breath stank of booze and chewing tobacco. Dusty let himself get drug out of the melee. The girl at the door yammered at them as they went by, but they ignored her. The moment they were outside they hustled their asses down to the pickup. It was colder than when they went in. They pounded on the windows, but Tweeter steadfastly refused to wake up. He was laying on the seat, wrapped in their coats, a faint smile on his lips. Dusty gingerly touched a knob forming on the back of his head. Toby started laughing.

"Well, I have to say little brother, pretty good dance."

They Should've Told You At The Door

Heil

"Heil Hitler."

They don't say it all the time, but once one gets started, the rest usually follow. For them it's as natural as breathing, a response just as automatic as saying hello or goodbye. It looks almost clownish, the shuffling masses, one arm held high in front of them. At first many of us laughed, it seemed so ridiculous, a few even humored them by doing it back, but over time even the most light-hearted amongst us began to feel sick. Then after a while even that went away, it became a normal part of our lives, just as normal as it was for them. Maybe it's bad to ignore it. I don't know, but I can't imagine what people would have us do. It's not like it's something we can control.

They do it everywhere. The hallways, the cafeteria, the dormitories, even the bathroom. It's disconcerting, but not in the way you would expect. It's not the action itself that is disconcerting, as I've said, we've all mostly gotten use to that, it's how the individuals do it differently that really sticks in one's mind. It's a little window into a secret world. A peephole that you're forced to look through, revealing exactly what type of person they were, and probably still are. For them, their surroundings don't matter anymore. They don't care, or probably even notice, what other people think. For them, it's their time and their place. You can tell a lot about someone by how they raise their hand.

Take Dieter and Werner for example. Both are kind men, easy going, the type that are always pleasant to be around. They both spend most of their time smiling and telling jokes to try to spread that smile to others. The only time they are serious is when they talk about sports scores. They grow uncomfortable with anything more serious. Nothing can get them down and they will happily avoid anything that might. When they salute and say the words, it's no different than a neighborly wave and greeting across a picket fence. There's no thought, no malice, just the application of a cultural norm.

Ursula is mostly the same way, though she seems to think of it as more of a silly joke, one of those strange things that everybody does that when you think about it, doesn't really make a whole lot of sense. However, she doesn't think about it much beyond that. Her salute is exuberant to the point of bordering mockery, the words always punctuated by an upward lilt at the end. In many ways she's an outsider, but an outsider willing to play the game in order to fit in.

Others seem to have a better understanding of what is going on. Karin and Manfred are good examples of this group. They do their best to hide their emotions, but they just can never quite seem to complete the illusion. A dead look behind the eyes. A tightening around the mouth. A tension along the spine. The salutes are stiff and the words bland, choked out the same as one would force down an unappetizing meal prepared by a loved one. Karin is better at hiding it than Manfred, you really have to look for the signs of distaste. Manfred just looks sick all of the time. He does what he has to do, but you can tell that it is twisting his innards. Killing him slowly. We are always kinder to Manfred than the others. We do what we can for him.

There are more. There is Karl and Klaus, their salutes and words loud and matter of fact. They are glad to be a part of something. They are proud of doing something bigger than themselves. For them, it is unimportant what that thing is, they just want to be part of history. For them, it's no different than the cheers at a soccer match. Thousands singing in unison, striving for a single goal. A member of the whole, hearts beating fast with the power of human unity.

Helga is the one that scares us, though it would be hard to understand just from looking at her. There is a fierceness about Helga when she does it. It's more to her than it is to the others. Part love and part lust. The taste of the words on her mouth are a passionate kiss. She quivers when she says them, bright flames burning in her eyes. There is no question, no doubt for her. She has seen the light and embraced it fully. It does not matter what happens, what those words and motions represent will always be the great love of her life. She looks like all the rest, one would never know the truth, until she does the salute.

We sit with them, and we care for them, it's what we've been paid to do. Sometimes we medicate them too. Maybe I shouldn't let it bother me so much. Maybe it should bother me more. I don't know. Whatever they might have once been, they are harmless now. Aging husks of a world now gone. Grim reminders of what once had been. They do not know what they do. They do not know where or when they are. They live in a limbo created by dementia. It was such a long time ago. Memories buried deep until now, exposed as the walls of senility collapse. For us it is just a job. We get to leave. We get to go out and have drinks with our friends. We get to live the lives they once had. We don't enjoy such things the way we used to. We know something that most would rather leave forgotten. They're back at the home, but we have them all around us. We see the seeds, planted in the soil of every ideology. They're out here with us. It frightens us.

All You Can Eat

Scott and the crew rolled into the Chang Sing at exactly five
o'clock, strolling between the two bronze lions on either side of
the door. The crew had been waiting in Big Head's Volvo
parked on the street for the past fifteen minutes. The Chang Sing
opened at noon for the lunch crowd, but the special didn't start
until five. There was no reason to come in before then. The
place was mostly empty, as was to be expected on an early
Tuesday evening, with just a middle aged Chinese man sitting by
himself in a booth. The wrinkled man had salt and pepper hair, a
heavy mustache in need of a trim, and a look that suggested he
had seen everything of interest long ago. He was smoking
despite the no smoking sign clearly emblazoned next to the door.
In front of him were piles of Renminbi, neat stacks of red, green,
yellow, and blue. When the boys walked in the man glanced at
them with a look of bored disapproval, then went back to his
counting, breaking away every few bills to watch Chinese soap
operas on the small TV hanging in a corner of the room.

Mrs. Hop came out of the kitchen to greet them, her mouth
smiling, but her eyes cold and calculating. She was a plump

woman with perfectly coiffed unnaturally black hair and a mincing gait. Mrs. Hop was of course not her name, but it's what all of the college kids called her, at least the less worldly ones who didn't care about such things. As for the more worldly ones, those who saw themselves as the forefront of a better and more understanding world, they called her nothing. Such people didn't come to the Chang Sing. Mrs. Hop grabbed four greasy menus and tilted her head slightly to the side.

"How many?"

Shooter snickered. Scott held up four fingers.

"Four."

Mrs. Hop led the way down the length of the restaurant to a booth near the far end and waited impatiently for the four boys to climb in. Scott and Big Head took the seats by the window. Shooter and Joe took the seats on the outside. Scott and Joe faced the length of the restaurant, the TV, and the back of the man counting the Renminbi. Big Head and Shooter faced a painting of a pagoda on the back wall. Mrs. Hop handed out the menus.

"Anything to drink?"

Three of the boys ordered Cokes. Shooter flashed his best smile at Mrs. Hop, his seated head only a few inches below her standing one.

"Tsingtao please."

"You have ID?"

"No."

"Then no beer."

Shooter never let his smile fade, even in defeat.

"Okay, Coke then, and a round of waters too."

Mrs. Hop nodded and moved off. Scott elbowed Joe to get his attention off the TV.

"How many again did Ken eat?"

"Seventy-four."

Big Head grunted and ran his hand down the front of his bright yellow sweatshirt emblazoned with an alpha, tau, and omega.

"Seventy-four. Shit. Bastard is crazy."

The man in the booth let out a hacking cough. Scott leaned in closer to Joe and lowered his voice.

"Did he get sick or anything?"

"He didn't puke or nothing, but he did look a little….."

The boys clammed up as Mrs. Hop minced her way back to them, four cokes and four waters pinched in each hand, the fingers inside the plastic cups. Shooter snickered again as she set them down.

"You know what you want?"

She started with Big Head and worked her way around, not bothering to write anything down. Big Head ordered a #4, Shooter a cup of hot and sour soup, and Joe a #11. When she got to Scott he let a pause build for dramatic effect.

"I'll take the special."

Mrs. Hop pursed her lips, forming a red ball in the middle of her pale face. It was only a momentary spasm before the smiling emotionless mask returned.

"No take outs on special."

"That's okay."

Mrs. Hop pursed her lips again, swept up the menu with her quick hands, and disappeared back into the kitchen. The boys leaned in towards each other again. Scott gestured towards Joe.

"You were saying."

"About what?"

"About Ken. So did he get sick?"

"Not that I know of. He looked a little green later on, but he didn't puke or anything, at least as far as I know."

Scott nodded to himself. Big Head smoothed down the front of his sweatshirt again.

"So you can't puke then."

Scott took in a deep breath and let it out.

"Guess not."

"Wouldn't be fair."

"I know man."

The table lapsed into silence. Joe watched the TV. Shooter turned part way round to do the same. Scott studied his hands. Big Head stared at the pagoda painting over Scott's shoulder. After about fifteen minutes Mrs. Hop yelled something in Chinese from the kitchen. The man at the booth yelled something back which was met by a louder retort. Grunting to himself, the man got up and went into the kitchen. They both came out carrying the boys' food. Big Head leaned in towards Scott.

"You ready for this shit?"

Scott pounded the table with his fist.

"Hell yeah."

Mrs. Hop and the man deposited the plates of food before the boys. Platters covered in globs of various colors varying from a dull brown to a bright pink for Joe and Big Head and a cup of soup for Shooter. In front of Scott landed a plate mostly covered with pork fried rice with ten large batter fried shrimp unceremoniously shoved in on one side. Scott gave the pair a cocky grin.

"You better keep that fryer going, because I'm hungry."

Without a word Mrs. Hop returned to the kitchen and the man returned to his booth. Joe and Big Head started shoveling in. Scott poured some soy sauce on his rice. Shooter pulled a piece of paper and pen from his coat pocket to start keeping track. Scott inhaled the shrimp one after another, tails and all. They weren't as big as they looked. They were mostly batter. It took less than a minute. Shooter dutifully put down ten marks on his paper. Scott rapped his knuckles on the table and raised his voice to be heard over the TV.

"More shrimp please."

The man at the other booth didn't even bother to turn around. Mrs. Hop came out of the kitchen and unhurriedly walked down to the table.

"What you want?"

"More shrimp please."

Mrs. Hop's eyes swept across the table, giving nothing away.

"You have to eat rice."

Everyone at the table stopped eating.

"Excuse me?"

"You have to eat rice."

Scott glanced over at Joe.

"Did Ken have to eat the rice?"

Joe, smiling slyly, shook his head no. Mrs. Hop crossed her arms over her chest.

"New policy."

All eyes were on Scott. He gnawed his bottom lip a bit as he always did when he was thinking. Joe's smile was growing bigger.

"If you want to just......"

Scott motioned for him to shut up and then gestured towards Mrs. Hop.

"Okay. I'll finish the rice. Just bring me more shrimp."

Mrs. Hop turned and walked away. The boys huddled together. Big Head was glaring at Joe.

"You knew you son of a bitch. You fucking knew."

Joe glared back.

"Oh sure, how the hell was I supposed to know."

"You rotten....."

Scott waved his hands for silence.

"It's okay. I'll just eat the rice and we'll get on with it. Okay?"

The others nodded their ascent. Scott shoveled down the rice on his plate, finishing just as Mrs. Hop returned with another plate of shrimp and heaped up rice. Scott sucked down the new shrimp just as quickly as he had the first. Shooter added ten more ticks to his tally. With a flourish Scott banged the table again.

"More shrimp please."

Mrs. Hop came out of the kitchen and over to the table. Her smile was still in place, but her eyes were starting to look annoyed. She quickly surveyed the scene.

"You haven't finished rice."

Joe snorted back a laugh and Shooter snickered. Scott's gleeful adulation fell into a look of despair.

"I have to eat it every time?"

"Yes, every time."

Big Head was grinding his teeth.

"That's not really all you can eat shrimp then."

"You don't like it, go somewhere else."

The man at the other booth had turned in his seat to watch. Big Head looked ready to go off. Scott put his hand on the sleeve of his friend's sweatshirt.

"It's okay. It's okay."

Mrs. Hop nodded and headed back into the kitchen. The man in the other booth turned back to his counting and the TV. Scott stared stupidly at the mound of rice. Shooter patiently waited. Joe was openly grinning like an idiot. Big Head shot daggers at him.

"You dirty little son of a bitch!"

The exclamation echoed across the Chang Sing. The man glanced over his shoulder at the boys, gave them the evil eye, and then went back to ignoring them. Joe let loose a laugh. Shooter moved to put away his pen and paper.

"Well, I guess that's it then."

Scott motioned for him to stop.

"What if Big Head eats the rice?"

Joe shook his head emphatically.

"No way."

"Ken didn't have to eat all the damn rice."

Shooter thought about it for a moment, snickered to himself, and nodded his head.

"Okay, that's fair."

Scott and Big Head grinned. Joe scowled. Big Head kept his voice at a conspiratorial low.

"Just put it on top of the rice on my plate. Don't let them see you do it."

Scott raised his plate and scraped the rice onto Big Head's plate, careful not to scratch the fork along the ceramic. Big Head shoveled in the rice with a practiced ease. When the pile of rice on Big Head's plate was close to where it had started Scott knocked on the table triumphantly.

"More shrimp please."

Mrs. Hop brought out another plate heaped high with rice and ten shrimp. Scott and Big Head repeated the process. Shooter put ten more marks down on the paper. The process repeated itself five more times. Mrs. Hop eyed the table each time she came out, taking it all in, looking for inconsistencies. Her perfectly placed smile was beginning to twitch at the corners when she removed Joe's platter and Shooter's soup cup. The amount of rice on the plates began to grow, transforming from mounds to heaps to mountains. Seventy slash marks covered Shooter's paper. Scott was looking a little green. Big Head looked downright ill. He moved his fork into the massive pile, took a bite, and then put his fork onto the table.

"I'm sorry man. I can't eat anymore."

Scott shoved the last shrimp, number seventy, into his mouth.

"C'mon buddy, we're so close."

"Sorry man. I just can't. I feel like I got a boulder in my gut."

Scott looked at the other two boys in the booth imploringly.

"Couldn't one of you guys?"

Shooter snickered.

"Sorry, I'm just the observer."

Joe was smiling malevolently.

"No way in hell."

Big Head belched loudly.

"I'm going to puke."

Big Head desperately shoved at Shooter who obligingly got out of the way as quickly as he could. Big Head rushed to the single hole bathroom over by the door, the demands of his gut overtaking any chance of pride or subtlety. He was not quiet about it. The noise attracted Mrs. Hop who glided out of the kitchen and over to the booth, the glint of victory in her eyes.

"You need check?"

Scott shook his head.

"No thank you, I'm not finished yet."

Mrs. Hop's lips pursed again, but only for a moment. A plump hand reached over and grabbed Big Head's plate. She scrutinized it with a practiced air and then leaned in as though they were all fellow conspirators.

"Your friend been eating your rice?"

Scott's face remained as blank as hers.

"No."

"That a lot of rice for one so scrawny."

"I have a hollow leg."

Shooter snickered. Mrs. Hop's smile was the only part of her not radiating malevolence. She turned and her mincing steps carried her back toward the kitchen. When she drew near the man in the other booth she barked at him in Chinese. His entire body flinched. He answered quietly and she barked at him again. With an audible sigh he turned so he was sitting sideways in the booth, his face half turned toward the boys. Satisfied, Mrs. Hop went back into the kitchen. Seeing no other option, Scott dug in. He gagged at the first bite so made the second one smaller. He picked at it slowly, but surely. Scott belched. His

gut churned and let out an unsettled rumble, but he kept at it.
Big Head came out of the bathroom. Shooter got up to let him
back in.

The man in the booth grew bored. He turned his head back
toward the TV, glancing over from time to time to check. The
longer it went the farther apart grew the glances. Scott carefully
picked up his plate. With slow and easy movements he put it
down by his lap and upended the contents onto the floor.
Shooter snickered. Joe began to say something, but Big Head
shot him a glance that told him to shut up or else. Big Head
nodded at Scott, smiling like a loon, his eyes filled with elation.
Scott carefully lifted the plate back onto the table. He rapped his
fist on the table victoriously.

"More shrimp please."

Mrs. Hop came out of the kitchen. She took in the scene
from afar. She sucked in a breath between her teeth and said
something quietly to the man in the booth who answered at a
more normal tone. She said something sharply back and then
slipped back into the kitchen. She came back out a few minutes
later, her smile never before so obviously forced. Her tiny
footsteps swept her forward like a centipede. She laid the plate
down in front of Scott, five shrimp amongst the overflowing
rice. Big Head motioned toward it.

"There's only five."

Mrs. Hop swept her black gaze onto Big Head. Her high
voice was almost a bark.

"Shrimp expensive. We can't afford to waste. He finish
these, he get more."

Scott motioned for his friend to be silent. He began eating
the shrimp, Shooter adding them to the tally the moment each
was swallowed. Mrs. Hop didn't leave. She stood over them, a
leering demon, her eyes skittering like spiders across them,
looking for any proof of malfeasance. Shooter marked the
seventy-third shrimp. Joe turned in the seat as though to get out.

Mrs. Hop's eyes shot into the gap where his legs had once been. Her hands exploded downward onto the tabletop with sudden ferocity. She screamed something shrilly in Chinese before regaining enough control to express herself in the language the boys could understand.

"Rice on floor."

There was something that sounded like Chinese curses. "Rice on floor. You cheat me. You cheat me."

Joe and Shooter popped out of the booth like jack in the boxes. Big Head leaned as far back from the ferocity as he could. The man in the other booth calmly rose, went into the kitchen, and returned with a large pipe wrench in his hand. Scott sat calmly, one closed fist on the table.

"Okay. Okay. We'll just pay and go."

Mrs. Hop was nearly bouncing with anger.

"You pay and you go. You pay and you go."

"Okay. Okay."

Scott looked at Big Head out of the corner of his eye.

"You got this buddy? We'll even up at the house?"

Big Head nodded, his hand reaching for his wallet.

"Yeah, no problem, no problem at all."

Mrs. Hop went and got the bill. She watched Big Head count the money and lay it before her. She counted it again to make sure. She didn't move to bring them any change. She motioned toward the door.

"Get out. You banned. Never again."

The boys filed out into the cool night air. They said nothing until they got into Big Head's Volvo and safely pulled away. Joe started laughing in the backseat. A deep condescending laugh of triumph. Big Head glared at him through the rearview mirror.

"What the fucks so funny?"

"Seventy-three. Scott only ate seventy-three."

Big Head slammed his hand on the steering wheel.

"Fuck."

Seated in the back with Joe, Scott didn't say anything. He just smiled and opened his fist. Two crushed shrimp sat on his greasy palm. With a deliberate air he popped the two crustaceans into his mouth, chewed slowly, and swallowed with the greatest of theatrics. Joe was frowning. Shooter snickered.

"Winner winner."

The Gorge

There are a lot of people posting about the fire in the
Columbia Gorge and how terrible and heartbreaking it is to see
the destruction of places so many have loved. It's true, it is
heartbreaking, but I for one am also looking forward to what is
to come. Fires can cause destruction, but they can't really
destroy. No matter what is consumed, the foundations remain.
Existence is made of such things, and from them and the change
they wrought come some of the most beautiful moments we will
ever see. How many of us will curse the ashen remains while
they stand starkly in the moonlight? How many will cry over
blackened soil as green sprouts re-emerge? How many will miss
the wonderment of what is to happen? Each stage of the return
unique. Each amazing and spellbinding in its own way. Each
able to take one's breath away. It's true, the return will take
much time. Many of us will be old and gray by the time it is
finished, and even then it will not be the same. It will never be
the same, but such is life. Someday children will stand next to a
rotting sign describing the fire of 2017, and they will not
understand it as you do, for they never got to see the

transformation from death to life. A world of morphing reality. The only limitation is our own inability to view the world past our own short existence. Nature cares little for our point of view. Where others saw one Gorge, we will see hundreds if not thousands. Each one unique. Each beautiful if looked at in the right way, free of despair for what once had been. So cry today my friends. Weep for what has been lost. But open your eyes and raise your heads tomorrow, for what is coming is not something to be missed.

The Second Best Movie Review Ever

I knew it was a popular movie, so I really shouldn't have been surprised at the number of people there, but it was still kind of startling to see that many people in the theater. I mean, it was only half full, but it was an all right sized theater and also ten in the morning on a Friday. Understandably it was a little bit of a shock, and I'm not proud to say that my thoughts were less than positive towards my fellow theatergoers, mostly in the line of look at these unemployed losers, which is kind of ridiculous given that I myself am currently unemployed. To be fair, not everyone in the theater was a victim of my brain's unproven assertion. For whatever reason my subconscious gave a pass to everyone of Hispanic heritage, apparently because they probably worked nights or something, which upon closer inspection, really doesn't make me seem like any better of a person. Obviously, I have some implicit bias issues to work through, but that's not really what we're here to talk about today.

Going to the movie theater alone at ten in the morning does have its advantages, one of the most important being you can choose a seat where nobody is sitting on either side, thus giving you full access to two armrests. Unfortunately, this advantage is often lost when some less than socially conscious person decides that the seat next to you is the perfect vantage point for the movie, despite the fact that half the damn seats in the theater are still available. In my case this ne'er-do-well was a man named Ken, which given the fact I never spoke to him is most likely not his real name, but let's just call him Ken anyways. Aside from lacking an understanding of basic decorum, Ken also happened to be a rather rotund man with an odor best described as middle school football locker room after the big game. So you know, not pleasant. Now to be fair to Ken, I could've totally just moved seats. In fact, there were two open seats right next to me on my right. However, my brain, being a jerk with a martyr complex, decided that moving seats would probably insult Ken, a man I hadn't even made eye contact with. Such is the way of things.

Now sitting next to the smelly guy in the theater is unpleasant, but not ruinous in the grand scheme of things. No, that honor goes to the person three seats to my right who felt the need to keep checking their phone clear through the damn movie. Now many of you are probably thinking, just tell the jerk to cut it out, which under normal circumstances is a stance I would wholly agree with. However, this was no ordinary circumstance. First, by the light of the phone I could see enough of the woman's features to pick up the exuded sense that this was a person who would likely relish the opportunity of some type of confrontation. I don't know how to describe it, but she just seemed like the type who would likely respond to a polite request with loud and creative curses slung in my general direction. Second, and more importantly, she was obviously about eight to nine months pregnant, resting her phone on the swell of her belly as pregnant women often do.

I'm no expert in the ways of the world, but I'm pretty sure that even in a situation where one is clearly in the right, the general population will not look upon you as the good guy when involved in an altercation with a pregnant woman. That is just not the way the world works. The final nail in me saying something was the presence of a man on her far side who I can only assume was her husband/lover/whatever. Sure, the guy looked like a drowned rat, but even drowned rats get unpredictable when it comes to defending their young. No, sometimes the world just pisses in your Pepsi, and it's just best to accept it.

The first time she checked her phone I got cranky, but I told myself to relax because life is short enough as it is. The second time I went with the assumption that she might have a very good reason to be checking her phone at such a time. I don't know, maybe her out of the womb kids were with a new babysitter of questionable reliability, or maybe her grandmama was having surgery or something and she needed to come see a movie to distract herself while she waited. The third time destroyed any such peace rendering suppositions. The third time was when I managed to see what she was doing. She was scrolling through Facebook. Not a quick check for messages or updates. No, this was a slow and gentle slide of the finger as she moved through the newsfeed, stopping for the occasional click of the like button, allowing long seconds of brightness to drag on as she considered which emoji would be most appropriate. This was no circumstance creating an unfortunate need. This was pure addiction.

Pure wrath overwhelmed me with the realization. The dark parts of my soul imagined someone punching her in the face, not me obviously, but someone. Such thoughts horrified me to the point where I forced myself to let it go, but then the fourth time came and I decided I could take it no more. All I needed was another person. Someone where it just wasn't me. Someone feeling the same annoyance as myself. My casual glances around the darkened theater revealed few candidates. The only one especially close to the action was Ken, and my stinky friend seemed oblivious to such things, leaning to the left as far as his girth allowed as though to be farther away from the issue. If I did anything it would just be me alone. It couldn't be a solo mission.

The fifth time happened. I couldn't allow such a monstrous abuse of my theater going enjoyment to continue. I swore to myself that she had one more chance. One more opportunity to do right before I unleashed the fury upon her for her indiscretion. I'm not proud, but I must admit part of me relished the coming storm. The dark portion within all of us impatiently waited for the taste of the sweet words upon my lips. Soon it would happen. The monkey on her back would force her hand as surely as it had before. No more would the righteous be trampled. The vision of my actions filled my mind. I'd lean over and glare. I'd clear my throat. I'd tell her to turn off that mother fucking phone. Who cares about the consequences? Who cares about how things end? It would all be worth it.

Luckily, no such thing ever happened. My musings ended as they were, as just pure fantasy. The movie came to an end. The madness collapsed with the start of the credits. I had to get out of there. I had to leave before I said something I'd regret. I pushed past the phone abuser and her squeeze. I escaped through the exit, down the hallway, and through the glass doors into the noon time sun. It was only then that I dared look back, my eyes searching through the glass for my nemesis. I saw them coming down the hall. That's when I discovered that what I had thought to be a pregnant woman in the darkness was actually an effeminate man with a beer belly in the light of day. It was too late to go back. The door had already closed. Not wanting to be one of those people who wait at exits to rage at people, I retreated to my car and headed home. It was only then that I realized that the shirt I was wearing was the same one that I had worn running the night before. Sorry about that Ken. I guess we were both the stinky ones.

Anyways, Deadpool 2, four out of five stars, well worth the watch.

Misogynists and Bigots

Oh good, I was waiting for the time to double down on the assumption that all of middle America is filled with nothing but religious fundamentalist homophobic racists. Lord knows it's much easier than forcing oneself to do a little introspection on how one's own group may have helped lead to the tom fuckery that is Trump.

Look, I'm not saying that such people don't exist, they most certainly do. However, it's not like the super religious, racists, homophobes, and/or misogynists suddenly just popped out of the woodwork, having not voted for the past decade, waiting for someone like Trump to come lead them out into the light. These asshats have been voting in every election, and buddy, it's not too far to go out on a limb to guess they probably haven't been voting Democrat.

So, if the asshats as described have always been voting Republican, it forces the question, can we really blame them for Trump winning? If not them, then who? Well, looking at data shows that Trump had his biggest gains (when compared to the 2012 presidential election) amongst the poor and less educated.

So, there you go, it was those poor dumb ass rubes. Guess we can say fuck them. Oh wait, those were the same poor uneducated rubes who won Obama the election in 2008 and 2012. Hmmm....well shit, guess this is a little more complicated than some binary worldview of us versus them, with them being a bunch of ignorant caricatures who only make choices based on stupidity and/or just being just plain terrible.

So wait, why would a bunch of people who voted heavily for Obama suddenly shift their weight to a nut job like Trump? Well, why did they vote for Obama? Remember all that stuff about hope? He promised a better world for everyone. Well, bad news, that didn't really work out for everyone. Don't get me wrong, we've made some great strides over the past eight years. Gays can get married, we're having some serious discussions on race issues, a bunch of people got healthcare, and the economy has been recovering. Oh wait, scratch that last one, the economy has only been recovering in certain areas and for certain groups. There's a lot of folks (rural areas and minorities too) that haven't been doing so hot, and in some cases, have actually been doing worse. News flash, economic growth is lower and unemployment is higher in the rural and suburban areas compared to the urban ones.

Again, not saying that there aren't some pretty terrible people out there, but maybe we should also consider that there are also a bunch of desperate people too, people so desperate they're willing to overlook how terrible of a person Trump is for even the slim hope of change to the status quo. If you're drowning, the fact that the only person throwing you a life preserver is making racist comments is not all that important. Sure, he could be lying through his teeth, promising the best life preserver ever, a life preserver made out of gold, but when the other person is pretty much saying shut up and stop whining, it's not hard to imagine what the result will be.

I'm sorry for the rant buddy, but damn it, things are going to be pretty shitty for the next four years, and there's a pretty good chance they're going to be shitty even longer if we all bury our heads in the sand and continue pretending that the other side is a bunch of moronic buffoons. We need to strip off the labels and start listening and understanding. Does that mean you have to agree with them? Hell no, but you sure as hell aren't going to change a lot of minds if you don't understand where they're coming from. Grouping everyone who voted for Trump into the fundamentalist misogynist/racist/homophobe group makes about as much sense as lumping every anti-Trump protester in with the window busting anarchists.

They Should've Told You At The Door

Landlady

There was a bit of a wait between meetings, so I got myself close to the next one before finding a box store parking lot to hunker down in. I parked near the back, out of the way of the crowds hustling in and out of the Canadian Tire, intermittently turning on and off the engine. Though it was summer it was chilly, but I didn't want to waste too much gas. Such things cost money. It was far cheaper to wrap myself in my coat and last as long as I could, fingering my way through my book, occasionally hitting the button on the radio to illuminate the time. I was supposed to be there at three. It would be the fourth house I would look at.

Number one had been a duplex inhabited by a pretty blonde around my own age. The place was clean and she had seemed nice enough, but throughout the interview she had given me the wary look that the lovely always give a member of my gender when met via Craigslist. I must admit that I had given her the once over, for at the age of twenty-four it's almost an unconscious reaction, and judging by how she watched me I was not as subtle as I should've been. It had been a while. I was out

113

of practice. To be fair, she gave me the once over as well, though I doubt for similar reasons. Hers was a more cursory inspection and assessment. Perhaps there was a part of me that wished otherwise, the part that felt atrophied by unuse, but I've long ago accepted that I'm not of the body type that turns heads. The conversation itself was pleasant enough, but it ended with the I'll think about it and let you know phrasing that told me that it was a definitive no. Such is the way of the world.

Numbers two and three weren't really worth mentioning. Number two involved a dank basement, its upstairs owner that strange breed of hairy potbellied man that seems to proliferate in the Great White North despite a total abhorrence to the wearing of shirts regardless of the outside weather. The thought of seeing his leathery brown nipples plumped to their full potential by the cold and a belly button quite literally overflowing with lints of blue and green everyday was enough to convince me to move on. Number three was an overpriced one bedroom apartment, cheaply made, but shined to a high gloss, with every square inch of floor covered by the repetitive swirling of artificial hardwood. The tour ended in the bathroom where it was difficult not to notice a massive turd serenely sitting in the toilet, which the prospective landlord casually flushed down without missing a beat. There was a fourth house as well, though I didn't count it since I never went in. The house was a ruin that stood out starkly from the well manicured world around it, a sharp middle finger against all levels of conformity. My gut made its inclination known and I followed obediently, slowing down only enough to confirm the address.

With a day of looking under my belt I was left with just one more. One last opportunity before making the half hour drive back south to Calgary where I was living on the floor of my cousin's and his fiancé's small five hundred square foot high rise apartment in downtown. A place where after two weeks even the bonds of familial ties were beginning to grow thin. Which is of course fair. I wouldn't want me living on my floor for long periods of time either. Hitting the radio button again the clock glowed 2:45. Careful to mark the stopping place in my book with a dollar bill, I started the car and headed out on my way.

The route was a maze of matching shiny vinyl houses lined up perfectly like pupils in preparatory school along streets with names like Silver Springs, Stonebridge, and Creek Gardens. The city of Airdrie was a cookie cutter affair of suburbia. A shifting labyrinth of curving boulevards which gave out without warning, forcing numerous retreats and realignments. Not a single tree was more than twelve feet high, though they would likely all be magnificent bastards by the time the occasional child seen playing managed to scrape together their own identical dream.

The house itself was not the biggest on the block, but neither was it the smallest. It was a nice two story affair, white paint with blue trim, with no territorial fences dividing one set of grass and bushes from the other, and the garage hidden in the back along a graveled alley. I parked across the street and walked over, the steps of the front porch creaking under my shoes, mingling with the musical tinkle of wood chimes next door. I rang the doorbell and took a step back. I'm a tall man and my coat makes me look bigger than I actually am. I smiled when the woman answered the door, a gesture she returned in kind.

"Hello," I said, "I'm here about the room to rent."

"Of course," she answered, her bright blue eyes never breaking away from mine. "Right on time."

She was probably in her mid to late thirties, though such things are always hard for me to tell. She was a handsome woman, though not beautiful. An unkind person might even call her plain. She was starting to show the signs of age, faint crows feet around the eyes and a little more fat in the paunch and along the hind end. Her straight blonde hair was cut into a bob which framed her face and added roundness to the square set of her head.

"I always like to be punctual," I stated, letting my smile broaden in hopes of seeming to be a lighthearted fellow.

"It's appreciated, you wouldn't believe how many people show up to these things late. Please come in."

She pulled the door all the way open and I pulled open the screen, and with that I was swept inside to a small entryway divided from the living room proper by a short half wall. I must admit that I admired her back in a way that decorum didn't allow me with her front, but I hid it well when she turned and blocked my way.

"Would you please take off your shoes?"

It was phrased as a question, but her tone gave no hints of it being a request. I dutifully leaned down and untied my laces, rolling up my jeans so I wouldn't tread upon the hem. She watched the entire process silently, her eyes never breaking away, leaving me feeling pressed down by the gaze of a power from up on high. When I rose, she took a step back in order to give me full entry and gestured for me to sit on a cream colored couch.

"Would you like something to drink? Water? Pop? Beer?"

My senses flickered at the mention of beer, but I thought it better to put my best foot forward.

"A pop would be fine as long as it isn't diet."

Her eyes squinted a little in a way that brought out her crows feet.

"I'm having a beer."

The suggestion was obvious, but again the tone didn't suggest a choice in the matter.

"I'll have a beer too then."

"Good, one always hates to drink alone."

She walked through the dining room and out to the kitchen, all visible via open double doors. I took a moment to enjoy the view again and then gazed about my surroundings. It was a standard living room. Couch, chairs, end tables, coffee table, a few potted plants, bookshelves built into the wall on either side of a fireplace, and a TV in its nook in a corner. Everything was set just right, the quality all more towards the higher end. There were no signs of pop culture or personal knick knacks, except for a few photo albums tucked low on a bottom shelf next to an Atlas. The other books on the shelves were hardbacks with the colorful jackets removed, their number balanced carefully with a few decorative pieces of varying sizes and types. The photos were all landscapes or close ups of plants. The carpet was a mix of tans and browns. Matching curtains hung from stately rods, framing the windows. It was clean to the point that she was either persnickety about such things or had the money to hire someone to do it for her on a regular basis.

She returned with a gliding step, moving along while still not being in a hurry. She leaned over to hand me my beer and then took a seat on the other end of the couch, turning her whole body to face me, tucking her legs up beneath her. I could feel her watching me with a steady line as I took a drink and studied the label. It was something called Rickards White, not an instant favorite, but palatable. She waited patiently for me to get up the nerve to look back at her and then got to business without delay.

"I think it's good for us to get to know each other. That way we'll see whether or not this is going to work."

I nodded my head in agreement. The questions came one after another, a steady cadence of inquiry with the feel of a job interview. Where was I from? What was I doing in Alberta? Where did I get my education? What did I like to do? How many siblings did I have? How long was I going to be in Canada? I answered as best I could, smiling and trying to throw in the occasional joke. I felt like I should ask my own questions, but I didn't, rendered incapable by a brash display of confidence I knew I would never be able to match. Her eyes were on me the entire time, her gaze never wavering but for the occasional shift for her to take a drink of beer. Two blue beams skewering me like an insect beneath a microscope. Studying every nook and crevasse to ascertain exactly what type of bug I was. The house was warm, so I took off my jacket, every movement feeling jerky and unnatural. Every breath and beat of my heart was a noticeable echoing shudder across my form. I could feel every movement of my face as I answered her questions. Every slip of my tongue. Again and again I retreated from the ferocity of her gaze, falling back to the safe havens of the less intimidating comforts of the world around us and the sweet liquid release of my beer.

Then it was done. The questions stopped coming and for a moment she broke away, staring upward at the ceiling as though through it, the husk before her completely forgotten for a moment before her gaze came back down and the flow of information reversed itself. She began to tell me about the neighborhood, the town, and the area in general. She mentioned the rent. The terms. A stately queen upon her throne, surrounded by the finery she had collected as an upper mid-level executive of a company that likely made something or did something of some importance. This was her kingdom, and it must be recognized that I was the one meekly asking for entrance. I tried to face up to it again. Tried to assert some kind of foothold, but fell back, first from her eyes to her mouth, then from her mouth to her beer on the coffee table, resting for another attempt.

Her words kept coming, but increasingly they drifted through without sticking, my mind completely overwhelmed with the task of controlling every little minutia of my existence, lest any movement or gesture be judged as lacking. With a sudden horror I found myself wondering what her nipples looked like. What color were they? What shape? What size? I desperately tried to stifle the stray thought, but it roared back, doubling in strength and size. I could feel my eyes wandering toward the small globes beneath her shirt, delving through the cotton layers.

It spread like wildfire. No longer just nipples and the curve of a breast, but everything. The shape of her legs. The roundness of her ass. The line of her neck. The shape of her ears. The quick litheness of her hands as they tucked a strand of hair behind said ears. There was no safe place to look. No safe haven at all in her direction. I jerked away to the refuge of my beer. I could feel sweat glistening on my brow. The cadence of her voice changed to that of a question.

"Would you like a tour?"

I took a swig of my beer and held it in my hands. For a brief moment I thought I caught a glint of amusement in her eyes, but when I looked again they were all business.

"Of course."

She rose and I obediently followed. My eyes darted from one place to the next. I refused to let them rest anywhere for long, fearing the danger of prolonged exposure. From the living room we went into the dining room. A heavy table surrounded by twelve sturdy chairs. A cabinet in the corner holding fine dinnerware. Still lifes of fruits and breads hung on the walls in elaborate wooden frames. Her long fingers intimately brushed against the backs of chairs as she walked past them.

"I hold a dinner party about once a month. You'd enjoy them. Lots of interesting conversation."

The idea of dinner parties held little interest for me, but I bit my tongue. She led me into the kitchen like a balloon on a string. Its counters were a dark granite with a matching stone facade on the floor. The sink as much decoration as tool. The appliances chrome, buffed to a high shine. There were no magnets on the refrigerator. No pictures, wedding invites, or grocery lists. I drank the last of my beer and stomped the thoughts bubbling through me into the ground, crushing them beneath my heel. The illusion of the temptress before me collapsed back into the reality of a woman simply renting out a room. Silently cursing the shortcomings of my gender, I tapped the glass of the bottle on the granite of the counter.

"Where would you like me to leave the bottle?"

She broke from her rehearsed tour spiel and gestured toward where I had tapped.

"Just leave it there. Would you like another?"

I really didn't need another, but a brashness overtook me, a need to assert some kind of dominance whether it was proper or not.

"Sure."

She smiled and opened the fridge, pulling forth two bottles, one for me and one for herself. With a casual air she popped the tops with a church key from a drawer and handed over mine. Her fingers brushed mine as she did and I could feel the damnable thoughts of the living room rising once again, but I refused to let them. I squeezed them back into the deeps, focusing all of my brain power on listening to the words of her restarted tour, concentrating on the coldness of the beer flowing down my throat.

Off the kitchen there was a bathroom, but we merely brushed over it as a necessity without notable merit. The same treatment was given to the backyard and the garage. Back to the front we went and then up the stairs. Here at last was broken the formal facade. On the walls of the upstairs hall were rows of pictures of the house's mistress. Photos with friends, formal photos at banquets, photos of relatives living and dead, and vacation photos posed in front of stunning vistas. One of these was of her in a bikini, and though nothing of great attractiveness or note, I let my eyes linger on this one longer than the others, drinking in the portions of her currently hidden away, but breaking away before I was caught staring.

We did a cursory glance through the second bathroom, this one as well in good order, though not in the picture perfect sense of the first, for even with everything in its place it still looked lived in. The light was flicked on and off in rapid succession, and then without even a backward glance she moved on down the hall to an open door.

"And of course this would be your room."

I pulled up even and looked in but took a slight step back when I found another person already inside.

"This is of course Jacob. Like I said earlier, he's moving out next week."

He was a thin wiry boy of probably around twenty, sporting thick rimmed glasses, hair over the top of his ears, and a slight breakout across one cheek. To call him a boy was unkind given that I was only four years older than him, but I felt him to be a boy in comparison nonetheless. The room was dark with curtains across the one window and contained little more than a blanket covered mattress on the floor, a half filled duffel bag surrounded by scattered clothes, and a stack of paperback books of various genres. All together it resembled the den of some packrat, though looking back it seems somewhat of a subjective analysis coming from a man living on his cousin's floor.

"Hello," I said with a jaunty flare.

"Hello," Jacob answered, his voice flat and without emotion.

I poked my head into the room, but not for long, conscious as I was that it was still his space. I also didn't want to remain long in my possible predecessor's presence. He seemed a sullen sort, and his gaze reminded me of a dog who had been disciplined for growling at another dog that had entered its space. If the mistress of the household noticed any of it she chose to ignore it, instead cheerfully continuing on toward a closed door, me following like a tethered pet. She swung the door open with an aplomb and ushered me in.

"And this of course is my bedroom."

She said it with an air of finality that caught my notice, as though this was of course the natural place for any tour to end. It was a big airy room, brightly lit by the sun via two large windows on the end which looked out over the street. In one corner was a dresser with two photographs which I guessed were her mother and father. In another corner was an old style full length mirror on a stand. The centerpiece was the bed. An edifice with bed posts sticking up taller than my head, covered with a patterned white coverlet and offsetting throw pillows of various shades of dark green. The room was as tidy as the rest of the house, with such added small details as a bed skirt giving off a feel of class.

She fell silent for a moment, as if giving me a chance to drink it all in and then moved over to the bed to sit down, one leg crossed over the other. It was a tall bed, and her foot just barely touched the ground. She motioned for me to join her, which I did, though I felt awkward taking a seat on the bed of someone who might end up being my landlady. As soon as I was situated, we began in again, starting out with repeating the terms, but then shifting onto the subject of Jacob, his time as a tenant, where he was going, and where he had been. He was apparently a college student, but beyond that I really can't say, for I was quickly again becoming distracted.

It seemed to me as she spoke that she lent in closer, her hand dropping down next to mine, her fingers so close that I could feel the crackle of energy. She was staring at me intensely again, and though I tried to surmount it, again I fell back before her. My gaze traced the line of her mouth. My lips felt dry, so I licked them. I could see myself leaning closer. One smooth motion as though sliding down an inevitable hill. In a moment she'd be in my arms, her hands fumbling at my belt buckle. In the real world she said a joke, tapping my leg with her mirth, me dutifully laughing as well. I'd bend her over the bed. I'd pound her for all I was worth, my hand tugging on her bobbed hair, her yelling for me to go deeper and harder, begging me to not stop.

The bedroom door was open. I could see Jacob glance in as he left his own room, the same look still upon his face. He only paused for a moment, long enough for our eyes to meet, and then he moved away. I heard his footsteps retreat down the stairs, the front door open and close. My free hand was fumbling with the empty beer bottle. She brushed back the same apparently untrainable lock of hair. I'd be asleep in the room next to hers. How would it happen? How would it start? She was still talking, her eyes locked on me, never moving away. Her free hand was toying with her beer bottle as well, now just as empty as my own. I could feel myself lean in closer. I could see her eyes widen. The bottle dropping to the floor as her hand struck my face. Loud cursing as she hit me again and again, demanding that I get out. She was smiling at me, her eyes staring so intently. Such beautiful blue eyes. I didn't look away this time. She smiled at me. She was saying something. Good god what was she saying?

"Anything else?"

"No, nothing else that I can think of."

"All right. Well, let's both take a day to think about it and you can get back to me, but don't wait too long, I'm planning on having someone to fill it before Jacob leaves."

I nodded dumbly. She rose and headed for the stairs. I followed as demurely as a puppy. She took the beer bottle from me at the bottom of the stairs and took it and hers into the kitchen. I picked up my coat from the couch, went to the front door, and started lacing up my shoes. She came back out and leaned against the wall while she waited. I could feel her eyes tracing across me. When I rose she smiled and offered her hand.

"It was very nice to meet you."

I took it in mine. She had a good grip. It felt like it took longer than it should. I could see her on the couch, me on top of her, her hot breath in my ear, urging me on. I could feel the blood rushing to places I didn't want it to go.

"It was nice to meet you too."

123

Our hands dropped and I looked dumbly at her, the fantasies boiling feverishly in the background. She watched me, waiting. I had to do something.

"Well, have a good evening."

"You too."

I turned and went out the door. The screen clanged closed behind me. I could feel her watching me as I went down the porch steps. Watching me as I went down her walk. Watching me until the moment my foot left her property, and then she closed the door. I got in my car and drove the half hour back to downtown Calgary. I parked my car in the underground garage and rode the elevator to up near the top of the high rise. The apartment was empty when I got there. I went in the bathroom and did what I had to do to return to some sense of normalcy, of decency. I had her phone number written on a piece of paper. Her instructions echoed through my head. It all hung right there in front of me until with a sudden jerk it was all gone. Flushed away back into the nothingness from which it came.

My cousin and his fiance came home an hour later. He started cooking dinner while she sat down with me to watch TV. It was my cousin who broached the subject. Raising his voice from across the counter of the kitchenette.

"Get any good leads today?"

Her hand had been right next to mine. Our fingers practically touching. Her body leaning in closer towards mine as we sat upon her bed.

"No, nothing really. I've got some leads out towards Drumheller. I'm going to check them out tomorrow."

My cousin nodded and went back to his cooking.

St. Paddy's Day

Happy St. Patrick's Day. I know, some of you are probably just going to get sloppy drunk, and others are probably going to say how it's a crock of shit holiday, a holiday that back in Ireland was just about going to church. However, just because most of America gets blitzed on it, doesn't mean that it isn't still an important holiday that celebrates a very important aspect of our American culture.

St. Patrick's Day is a celebration of the Irish. The Irish, who were one of the largest groups of immigrants to ever come over to the United States. The Irish, who were one of the first groups of immigrants to the U.S. to ever face widespread prejudice and anti-immigrant laws, just because they practiced a different religion. The Irish, who came to America because they were trying to escape a homeland where they were treated like shit by an unjust government, a government that went as far as to refuse to prevent an entirely preventable famine, resulting in the genocide of over one million people. The Irish, who despite it all, overcame it all to find success and acceptance.

St. Patrick's Day is a celebration of overcoming adversity and tyranny to find a better life. It is a celebration of keeping traditional culture alive while at the same time integrating with American society as a whole. It is a celebration of immigrants. Raise a beer. St. Patrick's Day is a celebration of the best that America can be.

Stupido

"Oye, chico blanco, ¿qué diablos haces aquí?"

Standing at the entrance of her convenience store, the old woman yells after me, a younger woman looking over her shoulder. My stride has already carried me a half block past her place of business to the edge of the next street. If not for her tone, I probably wouldn't have stopped. Valparaiso, Chile's city by the sea, is full of people trying to sell you things. Aggressive hawkers of wares, fighting amongst each other for the limited resource of tourist interest and cash. I stop briefly and turn back. The old woman stretches out an imploring hand, gesturing for me to return.

"Ven aquí estúpido. Ven acá."

There is little in the convenience store that I want. The usual assortment of Coca-Cola, Super 8 candy bars, and Nestle ice cream. It is a pleasant day, the sun a bright eye staring down from a blue sky at the colorful city, its heat cooled by a stiff sea wind. The view along the rim is spectacular. The rim is a break in the flow of the city down the hill to the ocean. A spot too steep to build, creating a natural divide between the low and the high. Above me, a rainbow of buildings work their way up the hillsides. Below sit the tight streets of the commercial district and the bustling activity of the container port, the last small remnant of what this city of Neruda once was.

I arrived by bus from Santiago early that morning. A day trip to see what all the guidebooks called the last evidence of what Chile had once been. A romanticized version of what was assured to be a taste of an era of grandeur frozen in time by UNESCO decree. The area next to the bus stop was most definitely not the area advertised. It was tired and dusty. It looked like the kind of area you put a bus station. Such things are to be expected. Unperturbed, I shouldered my bag and headed out, bound for the city center.

The wires were the first thing I noticed. They hung like a spiderweb across the city, an artificial nervous system of electrical and telephone wires, connecting everything into a single united being. The poles were thick with wires. Some held hundreds of individual strands, stretching away through the sky, or coiled in large bunches that hung from their comrades. There were more than could ever be needed. The abandoned left in place. The new crammed in, using the old for the foundation of their installment. Nothing removed. Nothing forgotten. A visible complete history of our wired age.

The blocks of concrete, their graffiti covered facades broken only by roll up steel doors, gave way to the historical parts of the city. Wide avenues of asphalt turned into narrow streets of cobblestones, crowded in by tall buildings of turn of the century styles. Every doorway, window, and corner, decorated with a flourish of patterns and ornamentation. The narrow sidewalks were shared by crowds of tourists armed with cameras and packs of stray dogs, lying in the sun or happily trotting their way from group to group, looking for a bite to eat or a friendly pat from a stranger. Murals covered many of the walls, bright and avante garde, splashes of color upon the old world charm.

I climbed tight and turning stairways, each step painted another shade of the rainbow, up into a world of hostels, art shops, fine restaurants, and prayer flags. The city closed in, holding me tight with its sun warmed embrace, whispering promises of refuge from the modern age, caressing and pointing out the lost world of a simpler time, the illusion only broken by the new model cars rattling their way across the cobbles. Here the city seemed to say, here is what you have been looking for. Frolic in peace and listen to my ancient wisdom. See what the world can be. A place of peace and beauty, creation just for the sake of creation. I let it carry me to its heights. I let it put its arm around me and laughed with the joy that I was supposed to feel.

On one of the stairways I met a cat. A sleek gray beast with the collar and friendly disposition of ownership. He rubbed along my leg and I leaned down and stroked his fur, the buzzing of his purr making its way up my arm.

"Hola gato."

My new friend followed me halfway up the stairway, each step a mural that shifted as you moved upward. Near the top he turned and descended, leaving me to face the rim on my own. Old wrought iron railings, flecked by rust, protected seekers like me from falling down onto the rooftops below. The view was spectacular, the city stretching its way around the bright blue of the harbor. In the misty distance were the tall spires of the hotels and resorts along the beaches to the north. The sidewalks were crowded by booths of locals, selling identical knick-knacks as their neighbors. Scarves and hats of llama wool, miniature monuments beaten from copper, t-shirts emblazoned with the national flag, and tiny Easter Island heads made of stone. The eyes of the proprietors watched the tourists go past, attempting to use whatever magic they possessed to get their prey to turn and enter, eager to offer what they had available with mysterious smiles.

It was here that I discovered the elevators, or at least that is what they called them. Elsewhere they are called funiculars, though granted, being in Chile, it only seems fair to call them the same as the locals. Wooden cars climbing up and down seventy degree tracks with the assistance of cables and the weight of a twin. The interiors of the cars were simple affairs, painted or varnished, with a bench running down one side. For just a hundred pesos they were an alternative to the stairs. A steampunk masterpiece for those wanting to be fully enmeshed by the past. I decided to ride every single one.

Some were newer. Some older. Some were kept up quite well. Some not. Things tended to degrade the farther around the harbor I went. Up and down. Up and down. The final one was a ways from the others, on the other side of the port with its bustle of trucks and cranes moving containers back and forth. I walked past a square where streets and sidewalks merged into one, a hulking statue jutting its way into the sky atop a slab of concrete, the national flag held high. I rode the elevator to the top, and after paying a fee, worked my way through the Naval Museum, which offered little of interest outside the visual due to my inability to read Spanish. I went back out into the sunshine.

The sidewalks outside the Naval Museum were packed with the same purveyors and hawkers of knick-knacks and I felt a great need to break free. They inundated the place. A roiling mass of hungry eyes and flashing cameras. To the west was the world from which I came, between me and it a hillside covered in churches and residential domiciles. I decided to free myself for a time and make my way back from whence I came via walking along the rim. My mind made up, I headed down the street and quickly found myself outside the world of tourists, able to breathe easy once again.

The walk along the rim was not a straight shot, but rather a twisting maneuver, making its way around canyons where roads twisted their way upwards from the flats below. The sidewalk was not always the best, cracked and broken in places, but its condition was not a hindrance. The brightly painted buildings were of crumbling brick and rusted tin. Interiors guarded by shattered glass glued to the tops of walls. The streets were alive with the movement of cars and taxis, though at a much lower volume than the world below. The only kindred spirits were the locals, and they watched me pass, my bag slung over my shoulder, with a tired wary eye, the look given by a neighbor while watching a strange dog trot across their lawn. I liked it there. I reveled in its authenticity. The view was spectacular.

The woman motions once again.

"Ven aquí. Ven aquí ahora mismo."

There is something in their eyes, the old woman and the younger version behind her. They look worried. I turn and go back. The moment I do I see a small amount of relief cross both their faces.

"Este es un mal lugar para ti. No deberías estar aquí."

I look at the old woman, puzzled, unsure how to respond.

"I'm sorry. I don't speak Spanish."

The confusion appears to go two ways.

"Ingles?"

"Si, no Espanol."

The old woman's mouth tightens and she lets out a wary sigh. She points aggressively towards my intended route, shaking her head back and forth.

"No vayas por ese camino."

I look at the way I have been going.

"Don't go that way?"

It is evident she doesn't understand, so I point in the same direction and use one of the few Spanish words I definitely know.

"No?"

"Si."

I'm not really sure what to do with her instructions. It is obvious that my presence is troubling her. She points downward towards the flats.

"Vuelve abajo donde están los turistas."

I point down as well.

"You want me to go down?"

"Sí. Sal de aquí."

"Okay. Gracias."

There is definite relief in the eyes of both women. The older woman points downwards again, and mimes gripping a bag tightly in front of her. My hands shift my bag to around in front of me, and my grip replicates her suggestion into real life.

"Gracias."

The woman points again. I might be many things, but I'm not stupid. When a total stranger feels the need to say something, it often makes sense to listen. I retreat the way I've come, and at the first cross street take a right and head down the hill. A lonely cloud moves its way in front of the sun. The authenticity has taken an ugly turn. Bars on every window. Heavy duty screens on every door. The downward street cut short into an alley running perpendicular, the buildings on either side looming overhead. Two men stand on one end, talking in quiet voices. They turn when I appear. They have the eyes of cats, watching a wayward mouse caught out in the open. One reaches into his pocket. I turn and hustle the other way, walking fast, but with my shoulders high and ready. An old man enters the alley in front of me. He glances at me, turns his head, and mutters something under his breath.

I keep moving, not daring to stop. Back out onto another street, stretching its way down the hill. I move at a brisk pace, my body tensing with every passing person, every curious set of eyes. Down until I emerge back upon the plaza with the heroic statue upon its slab of concrete. A few bored tourists mill about. I stop outside a dirty looking restaurant on the corner to catch my breath. A fat woman emerges, a smile missing a few teeth arching its way across her face.

"You hungry? You eat?"

I wave my hand in polite dismissal.

"No thank you. No thank you."

The woman gestures once again, coaxing me towards entry. I move away down the street, back towards the remembered paradise where the tourists are packed the tightest. It is a paradise no more. It has revealed itself, an aging woman, her face slathered with far too much makeup, though not enough to hide the failing of her features. The buildings are crumbling and old, windows cracked and broken. Long needed repairs ignored or forgotten. Here and there are the ruined remains of structures that once had been. Skeletal frames baking in the sun. Graffiti covers everything, marring the walls and murals. No artistry, no effort, just quick and simple tags laid down with desperation, screaming to the world that the creator once existed. The sidewalks are covered in dog shit. It's everywhere. As I move, one of the producers of such organic land mines yawns and trots his way across the cobbled street, only to be run down by a passing taxi which does not slow. The tourists scream and snap photographs, but the locals pay no mind, not breaking their trodding gait, and not raising their heads to break the unending view of their own feet.

I move on as quickly as I can, making my way up the stairs to try and regain some semblance of my arrival. The faces of the vendors are contorted by twisted smiles that do not match their eyes. Masks pulled low to create some semblance of the reality their market demands. The curtain is pulled back. The world laid bare. The city is dying. Declared timeless, even as those same forces wear it away before my very eyes. This had once been a thriving place. Now it clings desperately to strings, selling its memories as it disintegrates piece by piece. The world I had seen had once been, but no more. It is all just a shadow. A dream of perfection that has never been. Unnerved, I climb the rainbow steps again, find a cafe, and drink several pisco sours.

Spaghetti Sauce

"Do you think Hoffman will put us in next game?"

Jared was looking out the window of the small trailer. Leo stopped scrubbing the cupboard door and looked up at his friend. The question seemed out of place. For a moment Leo was flummoxed to find an answer. Leo began to raise his hand to scratch his nose but stopped himself. Both boys were wearing yellow kitchen gloves.

"I don't know. Maybe."

Jared kept staring out the window, his gloved hands clasped behind his bent back. Leo dropped his sponge in the bucket of bleach water and rose up to look over Jared's shoulder. There was nothing, just the side of Jared's house across the top of his mother's Buick.

"Hoffman said your layups have improved. I'm betting he'll put you in next week."

Leo didn't answer. He just forced a half smile and then crouched back down to get back to work. The possibility of playing in next week's basketball game just wasn't that important to him. He wished Jared would quit staring out the

135

window and get back to work. They had a job to do, and Leo would rather get it done sooner than later. Leo pulled his sponge from the warm water and started scrubbing again.

It wasn't a big travel trailer. Sixteen by eight foot. A small bed hidden behind a sliding door, crammed behind an even tighter enclosed space around the toilet. The rest was taken up by a small kitchenette and a built-in dining table for two. The walls and cupboards were a beechwood veneer. The floor was yellowing linoleum. When they had first opened her up the table and floor had been covered with beer cans. Jared had insisted they bag them up for recycling. His dad had never been one for wasting nickels he claimed. Despite the harsh scent of bleach in the bucket, the smell in the trailer was still terrible. Bad enough to make Leo's stomach twinge. It's just spaghetti sauce he reminded himself.

It was everywhere. Dried splatters across the interior with a few random chunks mixed in. It covered the linoleum and cupboards in a spray down the length of the trailer, spreading outward from the table. The bench seats were vinyl, making them fairly easy to clean, but the curtains had to be thrown out, stained beyond hope. All that was left was the hard surfaces, but it had been nearly a week and was taking more elbow grease than expected.

Jared snorted and spit a loogie out the open door into the tall grass growing next to the fence on the edge of the driveway. He joined Leo on his hands and knees, took his sponge out of the water, and started scrubbing alongside. When their arms brushed Leo could feel a layer of clammy sweat on Jared's skin. They worked in silence that way for a little while until Jared threw his sponge back into the bucket and pulled himself around to sit in the doorway. Leo kept working, eradicating the red spots one by one. Jared snorted and spit again.

"Thanks for helping man."

Leo stopped long enough to look up.

"No problem."

"No, I mean really thanks, it means a lot. I don't think Mom would've been able to handle it."

Leo nodded and started scrubbing again. The dried droplets were everywhere.

"How's your mom doing?"

"Okay I guess. I don't know. I think she's still pretty upset with him."

Leo glanced over his shoulder at Jared. He was staring at nothing again. Leo kept working. It would never get done if they kept stopping.

"How about you?"

"I don't know. Probably better than having him living in the driveway."

There was something in Jared's tone that didn't sound right, but Leo didn't let himself think about it too much. He just concentrated on his work. He heard Jared spit again.

"I mean hell, it wasn't even like he was my real dad or something."

Leo wished Jared would just stop talking. It wasn't a fair wish, but he wished it nonetheless. At the very least maybe Leo could get him to change the subject.

"What do you think your mom's going to do with the trailer?"

"I don't know, sell it maybe, though I can't imagine who the hell would buy it around here. Probably we'll have to take it into the city or something."

Leo nodded though Jared couldn't see. The cupboard door he was working on looked clean, but he opened it just to make sure. There were a few splatters along the edge. He scrubbed them off and closed it.

"You know Amanda wanted to help, but I wouldn't let her."

"That girl loves the shit out of you."

"Yeah. I know."

"I've got to take a break."

Leo put his sponge in the bucket and Jared got out of his way so he could get out. It was cold outside, but Leo didn't mind. It felt good to be out in the fresh air. Jared sat back down in the doorway.

"It's just hard to believe the son of a bitch is gone. You know, he used to take me fishing all the time, get so damn drunk I'd have to drive us back home, even back when I just had a learners permit. Crazy son of a bitch."

Leo smiled a little bit. Jared continued, not noticing.

"He wasn't that bad. Even when he got to drinking too hard and Mom kicked him out. His heart was always in the right place."

Leo could see the tears in his friend's eyes so he politely turned away. It didn't feel quite right, but none of the other options felt right either. The sun was getting low. The exterior of the trailer didn't look too bad. It was actually in pretty good condition, all things considered, the white aluminum siding immaculate but for a small round hole at eye level, blown out from the inside.

Adventures In Dreamland With My Ex

I had a weird dream last night. That in itself isn't so strange. I have weird dreams all the time. Hell, the other night I dreamed that me and my mom were selling condoms at a kiosk at the mall. Nothing fancy or anything, we just had a big bowl of those cheap colored ones you get at the free clinic. We were charging five bucks for a handful. However many you could grab with one hand. Not that fair to people with little hands, but what can you do, it was just a fucking dream. There was one asshole that kept coming around. He paid his five bucks, took his handful, and then I saw him scoot right towards the hallway where the mall bathrooms are hidden away. Didn't even try to be sneaky about it. Sick son of a bitch.

Anyways, he comes back about five minutes later bitching that all the condoms broke, grabs another handful without paying, and scoots right off to the bathroom again. Left my mom speechless. Son of a bitch did it three times. We had no idea what to do. I wanted to confront the bastard, but my mom, not being all that confrontational, wanted nothing to do with him. It must have been her condom business because she won out in the end. When the guy came back the second time, I just kept my mouth shut.

The third time though, oh the third time, you wouldn't believe what the son of a bitch did. He actually had the balls to look at us and tell us he was going to report us for bad quality condoms. Can you believe that? I mean, c'mon, who's he going to report us to, the Bureau of Prophylactics? So I just looked at him and calmly told him that if we're doing anything wrong, it can't be near as bad as masturbating in public. The two of us stared at each other for a bit, then the corner of his mouth got to twitching, and suddenly he turned, ran away, and threw himself out a window. Shattered glass and everything. Second story at least. Crazy man, just fucking crazy. The whole thing shook me up pretty bad, so I went to the food court to get something to eat to help settle me down. That's where I ran into that girl I liked. You know, the one I told you about going on the date with. I didn't recognize her at first. She was all dressed up like she was some kind of high falutin business woman or something. I didn't realize it was her until after I woke up, but she knew who I was. Talked to me like we were old friends. I don't know. It felt really nice. Dreams are weird.

Anyways, that was nothing compared to my dream last night. The dream last night takes the cake. It started out alright. I was at some kind of seminar or something, I don't know, it looked like some kind of institute or museum. Beautiful day, warm weather, blue sky, big fluffy white clouds, lots of freshly mowed green grass next to this lake. Just nice stuff, though everything felt a little ominous. You know, like when you're watching a movie and you can just tell that something is off. Maybe it was the buildings. The museum, or whatever the hell it was, was built right next to the shore of the lake. It looked like some kind of moonbase, all futuristic like, with big domes and a dark metallic finish. There was the big building next to the lake and then another one out on an island maybe 300 yards out or so.

Don't ask me how I knew, but I knew there was an underground tunnel connecting them. Just one of those things. Dreams are weird. You get thrown into this whole new world and have to figure things out, but some stuff is just obvious.

There was some kind of festival going on. People everywhere, walking across the grass, going in and out of the buildings. Everyone seemed to be on their best behavior. The way people act when they're in a social situation with a lot of people they aren't exactly friends with, but whom they have to see all the time. Reserved. That's the word for it. Just a lot of people in groups chatting politely. Most people looked fairly young. I don't know, maybe it was a university or something. The smattering of old people there did have the look of professors. God only knows, it didn't really seem all that important to figure it out at the time.

I was standing in line for a food booth. There were a couple scattered over the grass around the building. This particular one was grilling skewers of meat on an open barbeque. The proprietor slash cook was an aging hippie woman with that kind of gray tightly curled hair that frizzes out and almost seems to float around one's head. Her clothes were oft patched jeans and a flowing colorful shirt with an untied drawstring at the neck, hence the overall hippy vibe, which was a little strange given the rabbits. Two small bunnies, one white and one brown, sat in a cage next to the barbeque. Each one would maybe fill your hand. The hippy lady had a cardboard sign attached to the cage with duct tape, on which was written in black marker, *YOU MIGHT AS WELL SEE YOUR LUNCH.* I don't know, it seemed all together a little too passive aggressive for a woman selling grilled meat skewers.

She was ahead of me a couple places in line. You know who I'm talking about. I didn't recognize her at first, what with her back turned to me, but there was something familiar in how she held herself, how she moved. She wasn't talking to anybody, just standing there, waiting her turn. When she turned her head a bit to look at something off to the side I knew it was her. A tall Greek statue with eyes the color of the ocean. She looked exactly the same as I remembered her, except for the hair. Her once brown hair was jet black, though to be fair, I already knew that. I'd seen it on her Facebook picture the time I got weak and typed her name into the search bar. It didn't get any farther than that. I never looked at her profile.

She didn't see me. At least I'm pretty sure she didn't. I watched her as she shuffled forward with the rest of us, drinking her all in. It's been five years since I've actually seen her. Five fucking years, and now there she was, in the flesh. I'll tell you, it paralyzed me seeing her like that. My brain just went on overload, overcome by memories, smiles and tears, terror and joy. Jesus Christ, so fucking much. I know, I know. I don't need to go into all that crap. You've heard it all before, but still, just like a sock in the gut. All that emotion. Jesus. Longing, anger, and that deep sadness they write fucking books about.

I didn't know what else to do, so I just watched her. She got up to the front of the line and saw the rabbits. I saw her whole fucking body tense. There was a look of hers I recognized, tension, but she must have gotten better at hiding it or something, because it faded pretty quick. I know what it was. She saw the rabbits in their cage with their morbid sign. Something like that would bother her. She moved away without getting a skewer. My eyes followed her. I wanted something. Something I've wanted for a long time. My body followed her too. There was this feeling deep in the pit of my stomach. It had been five fucking years, but there was something I felt I just had to say. Something that I've always wanted to say. *You need to apologize to me.* Finally get it out in the open. How would she react? Who the fuck knew with her. It's not the important part. I mean sure, it would definitely be nice to hear her apologize, even if it was just a dream. To finally hear her take some of the blame for everything that happened. To finally admit some god damn culpability. Throughout all the shit, you know how often I apologized? Damn, it seemed like hundreds of times by the end. It seemed like that's all I ever did, apologize. You know how often she apologized? I'll tell you. Zip, nada, a big fat zero. That's how many fucking times. Drove me fucking crazy. It would feel good to hear her apologize. Almost make all of it worth it. It wasn't the important part though. The important part was just being able to finally say it out loud. *You need to apologize to me.* God damn that would feel good.

So she headed off across the grass and into the building by the lakeshore, and I hustled my ass to catch up. The inside of the building was ultra-modern, I think that's what they call it. You know, a lot of concrete, thin metal, and neutral colors, kind of industrial in a stylistic sense, like a warehouse converted to overpriced living and office space for a tech company. It was kind of creepy inside. Bare walls, stark stairways with multiple landings, hallways with sudden sharp turns. The whole place felt like some kind of rodent maze. There were bright fluorescent lights, but widely spaced, leaving darkness in between. People milled about much the same as outside, drinks in hand, talking and laughing. I pushed my way through, desperate to catch her, but kept falling further behind.

We went down a set of ill-lit stairs. No art or decoration, just their width to suggest they were a more prominent route than the others. After several landings and ninety degree turns we emerged into what appeared to be a salt mine of sorts. It was darker down there. The temperature and a general sense of place suggested we were underground. The only light was a muted blue from a tunnel up ahead. The walls and random jutting outcroppings were bright white and sparkling, thousands of stars twinkling. The crowds had not dispersed at all, in fact they had grown thicker, especially in the tunnel. The tunnel was made of glass, holding back the underbelly of the lake. People were packed shoulder to shoulder, watching the fish, gasping in delight and surprise as more interesting specimens emerged from the murkiness and darted back away. I could see her on the other end of the tunnel. It took me a bit of time to squeeze past the mass, more than one individual bitching about a sharp elbow used to clear a path.

The other side of the tunnel had the same industrial chic look as earlier. It was a gift shop. Shelves filled with random nick-nacks. Books, posters, Lego sets, balls colored to look like the Earth, a selection of stick horses, and all sorts of other crap with no rhyme or reason, providing no clue or context. A small thin woman in a blue polo stood behind a cash register balanced on a small counter. Her clones roamed amongst those browsing through the collection, eyes alert for anyone thinking about stealing.

My eyes took it all in until they found her. She was standing near a tall shelf by the wall, her back turned to me. I made my way over, my guts churning with a cocktail of one part terror and two parts needing to say what I needed to say. I had no idea what I was going to say. How do you start something like that? You just don't blurt it out. What was I supposed to say first? I didn't want to be an asshole about it. This wasn't about making her feel like shit. I just wanted to assert my own emotions back into everything. I just wanted to show that I had been hurt too, that I was just as much of a person as she was. God damn she looked good. It was distracting to look at her. As I pulled alongside, I let my eyes focus on the shelf in front of me.

Battle Masters. I hadn't seen it in years, not since I was a kid. It was a board game. Okay, more of a big mat you laid out on the ground on which you moved around plastic army units, fighting it out via rolls of a handful of dice. The units were fantasy based, noble knights versus vile orcs kind of stuff. I used to love playing it as a kid. Sometimes I'd get one of my brothers to play it with me, but most of the time I played it alone, enthralled by the stories in my head. I could see her out of the corner of my eye, but I couldn't seem to look away from the game. There were apparently add-ons to the original. Little plastic warriors and monsters that I'd never seen before. A whole world that had moved on after I had left it behind. She looked over and saw me. Even not looking at her I could tell she was shocked to see me. She said my name. Music in my ears. I started to turn my head. One of the blue shirted clones tapped on my shoulder. My head swung towards the tap. There was nothing there. I swung it back. She was gone. Not like walked away gone. Just gone. Disappeared.

It was like changing a channel. No warning. No flicker. One second I was in the gift shop, the next I was back outside, waiting in line for a meat skewer. None of it seemed weird. Apparently, such jumps were perfectly normal in the world that I found myself. I could see her moving away again, back towards the building. It was her, but her hair was a different color. Brown again, the natural shade, just as back when I had known her. I wasn't sure what to do. If I followed, was the same thing just going to happen again? I tell you, it was weird. Things seemed darker outside than they had before, though the sun was shining just as bright. I don't know. I don't know why I did what I did next. The two tiny bunnies sitting in their cage next to the barbeque looked scared. You could see it in their eyes. How long would it be until they were skewered? They were trembling, just like she used to tremble.

It wasn't much of a cage. Just a small one with a metal door on either end that could be raised up by hand, the same as the live animal traps my father used to use to catch raccoons, rats, and other such varmints. There was a handle on the top. I wanted to help them. I desperately wanted to help those poor little rabbits. I got out of line and started moving forward. Nobody said anything. I was quick. Quicker than I could ever be in real life. I grabbed the cage and I ran. The hippy woman screamed. The eyes of the crowd turned. I sprinted out towards the open meadows, out past where the grass had been mowed. The rabbits scrambled in their enclosure, pissing themselves with terror. The older professor looking people started yelling. The tone and fit began to give chase. I could feel her eyes on me. I could hear her yelling my name.

I ran like I had never run before. My heart spastically threw itself against the confines of my ribs. It was nothing but pure adrenaline and madness. For a moment I was free, flying with the birds, but then arms wrapped their way around my legs, and I was crashing back to the ground. They took the cage with the pissed covered rabbits away from me and left me lying bloody in the dirt. The cage was returned to the hippy lady, who clucked at them with delight before going back to her skewers. The people turned away, back to their drinks and inane conversations. She was still watching me from across the field. The only one. Hot tears rolled down my cheeks. I had failed to save the rabbits. I had failed. I wanted her to come over. I wanted her to take me in her arms and comfort me, but she didn't. She turned away and walked into the building. I rose up to follow. I still wanted to say it to her. I wanted her to know. I wanted to hear what she would say.

I was in line again. The world had changed again, though I was still just as broken and bruised. She wasn't there. Nobody was there. There was nobody ahead of me in line. The hippy woman smiled and asked how many I would like. The cooking meat smelled good. I could feel my mouth water. One of the rabbits moved in the cage. The rabbits. I had to save the rabbits. Somebody had to do something. I was the only one who seemed to care. The hippy woman never saw it coming. My foot kicked over the barbeque and she fell back, screaming in shock and surprise, maybe even a few hot coals burning her, though I hoped not. I grabbed the rabbit cage and I ran again. Not the same way as before. Not towards the untamed edge of the lawn.

146

No, towards the building. I was quicker this time around. People were too distracted by the kicked over barbeque to offer any more than a token resistance.

It was cooler inside the building. Much fewer people milling around than there had been before. I found a narrow set of stairs and started making my way upward. I ran and I ran until I could not run anymore and collapsed onto the hard concrete of the top landing. The rabbits were skittering around in their cage. Was it fear or relief? I don't know. It seemed like both at the same time. I pulled open the metal door and they emerged, one after another. They weren't rabbits. They were birds.

The birds were roughly the same size as the rabbits, just enough to fill your palms. They were still the same colors, one white and one brown. Both had narrow yellowish beaks, long as my index finger. The same length as their ears had been when they were rabbits. Neither seemed to be able to fly. They just teetered around on their short legs, like babies before they get a sense of balance. It was strange. Almost like the old picture which could be either the head of a rabbit or a bird, depending upon which way you looked at it. It was all just a matter of perspective. I took the transformation rather well.

I could hear steps down below. Someone was climbing the stairs. I didn't know what to do. I picked up the birds and ran down the hallway, lines of doors to either side. I picked one at random and opened it. There was nothing but darkness inside. The birds pecked at me, obviously not wanting to go in, but I could hear the steps getting closer, so I pushed them in, shut the door, and ran back towards the top landing. It was the old hippy woman coming up the stairs. She was stopping at every landing, pausing to catch her breath. Nobody else was with her. She arrived at the top landing just as I made it back myself. The cage sat empty on the ground between us. She leaned over and looked inside, gave a dejected sigh, and looked up at me.

"Excuse me, but have you seen any rabbits? They were in this cage earlier."

She didn't seem to recognize me.

"No."

The hippy woman let out a dejected sigh again.

"Do you know how this cage got up here?"

I tried to give my friendliest smile. I can't imagine it looked very good. I'm a terrible liar you know.

"No idea, it was up here when I got here."

"And how long have you been up here?"

"Oh, about half an hour."

"And no one else has been up here?"

"Not that I've seen."

I must have been a better liar than I thought. The old hippy woman let out another sigh, peered behind me up the hallway, picked up the cage, and then started back down the stairs. I waited until she went down a couple landings and then rushed back to the door where I had hidden the birds. It wasn't dark inside anymore. Light poured in from a window. The room was bare except for a couple of tables and chairs of metal, pressed wood, and laminate. The kind you find in classrooms. The birds were gone. There were no rabbits either. I didn't really care.

She was there, by the window, sitting in the sunlight, bathing her face in its warmth. She turned as I entered. Her smile seemed forced, but her eyes were warm. I stepped into the room, unsure what to say. She watched every step with a look bordering on indifference. I stopped in the middle, a table in between us. We were both silent. Say it screamed a voice in my head. Just fucking say it. She broke the silence first.

"It's been a long time."

The answer was automatic.

"Yes."

"How have you been?"

"Okay. How about you?"

"Okay."

Things fell back into silence. I could see myself saying it. I could feel the kiss of the words on my lips. I could feel myself moving forward, my arms wrapping around her, her arms wrapping around me, holding each other tight, hot tears pouring from my eyes. None of it happened. Neither of us moved. My mouth felt dry. I licked my lips, willing myself to do something. Anything. Just standing there was madness, but it seemed to be all that I was capable of. Here was my chance, maybe my only chance, and I was wasting it. Finally my voice emerged.

"Have you seen any birds?"

She brushed a lock of brown hair off her face. Her eyes broke away and roved across the room before coming to land on the fake wood of the tabletop in front of me.

"No."

"What about rabbits?"

"I don't want to talk about this."

"Okay."

Silence again. She was trembling. It was barely perceptible, but I could tell. I licked my lips. I forced the words forward.

"There's something I've been wanting to say."

She was no longer looking at me. Her large eyes were focused out the window.

"There's something going on outside."

She rose up on her long lithe legs. My hands squeezed tightly into fists.

"There's something I need to say."

She was gone in an instant. She moved past me like a breath of wind, a quick feeling of warmth as she passed. I turned to follow. By the time I reached the doorway she was already out of sight and headed down the stairs. My chest hurt. My legs hurt. My head hurt. It didn't matter. I followed the best I could. The building was empty. Everyone had gone outside to see. She wasn't outside.

People were clustered and watching. Some held hands, pulling each other close. The professors were marching forward in unison, their legs kicking high, almost goose-stepping their way forward. The front center professor was brandishing the cage. The two rabbits were inside. They marched forward and surrounded me. They glared at me as though I was a naughty child that needed to be reprimanded. The professor holding the cage had a thick gray beard. He stared at me with hard eyes.

"These aren't your rabbits. Do you understand?"

I felt weak. Tired. There were too many of them to fight. My voice was quiet and meek.

"Yes."

"Do you understand?"

I raised my voice, better to be heard throughout the crowd.

"Yes."

"Good. Don't try to take them again."

The column reformed and began to march again, legs kicking high. One of the professors in the middle, a man with a mustache, gave me a malevolent grin. A sign of special pleasure for my discomfort and what was soon to follow. They moved as a single mass back towards the barbeque and the old hippy woman. She stood, watching them approach in silence, a skewer in either hand. I couldn't watch. I turned and fled back inside. Across the empty wide open space of the main room. Down the stairs wider than the rest. Down into the darkness of the salt mine. There was nobody. Just me. Alone. I found the darkest corner and I sat down. Salt crystals scratched at my arms. Salt tears poured down my cheeks.

The sound of running feet filled the tunnel. A tall man. Alone. He looked to be about five years younger than me. He threw himself into the darkness next to me, squealed with fear when he noticed he was not alone, and then fell into a silence broken only by his heavy breathing. I looked at him and he raised a finger to his lips. A commotion filled the tunnel. A mass of humanity pushing forward sounds of fear, anger, and panic. They came like a wave, almost as if the glass walls had broken. They were more beasts than people. A conflagration of swinging limbs. They fought amongst each other as they came. Punching, kicking, gouging, but moving forward the entire time, their faces contorted into masks of horror.

I stood up and took a step forward, unsure. My spot mate clawed at my leg to try to pull me back down. They were on me in an instant. Several breaking away from the main pack trying to make its way up the stairs. They were crazed beyond reason. I had to defend myself. I pushed them back and did what I could. They were no longer human. Someone punched me in the back of the head. The man who had been hiding in the darkness with me. He punched me again, and while I was dazed, threw me backwards into the shadows. The mass sucked him in.

A terrible howling, the deafening sound of a tempest, came from the tunnel, pushed forward by the emerging maelstrom. It was larger than the rest. A mass of gray robes shaped like a person but in no way what it appeared. Those in the back ranks, those within reach, were flung aside with the ease of a child throwing a doll during a tantrum. It was horrifying to behold. The mass fell apart into a bloody crumpled mess as it moved forward. Its appendages seemed to stretch beyond their length to snatch the unlucky back into the slaughter. People screamed and others groaned. Body parts went flying. There was no fighting it. There was nothing that could be done. I saw the man that had hidden in the shadows with me lifted over the beast's head before being ripped in half. I curled myself up into as tight of a ball as I was able, praying for the shadows to hide me from the darkness before my eyes. It did not see me. It didn't pause. It moved up the stairs, wreaking havoc as it went.

The moment it passed the first landing I ran full speed through the tunnel. Its length was choked with smeared blood and grisly remains. Water leaked through several cracks.

Curious fish crowded around, peering into the strange world of those who breathe fresh air. What had once been a gift shop was ruined. The shelves were all tipped and the nick nacks thrown far and wide. The carnage was more spread out, but every bit as bad as in the tunnel and the salt mine. There was a stairway near the back. I moved towards it when I heard the groan. It was her. She was cowering behind the counter where the cash register had once stood. Her hair was blonde now, trimmed to a pixie cut. Her eyes were filled with fear. One cheek was bloody. I grabbed her by the hand and pulled her to her feet. I half drug her up the stairs.

"What was that?"

She didn't answer. She seemed damn near catatonic. All systems on, just nobody at the controls. The top of the stairs were different than everything else. Ostentatiousness by wasted space and bare bones gave way to the same through richly splendor. It was a waiting room of sorts. Mahogany paneled walls, big leather chairs and couches, oil paintings in ornate frames, and a large rosewood desk. I pushed her through the ornate door behind the desk, and entered the private world within.

The decorations looked much the same as the waiting room before, just larger and more grand. A monstrous desk filled one end. Windows punctured the wall, revealing the peaceful scene of blue sky and the dark water of the lake all around. The room was rigged with booby traps, or at least the type of booby traps that would be built by a child. Dozens of strings hung from the ceiling, attached to the walls in such a way that the wrong step in the wrong place would release them. At the end of each string was a myriad of objects. Letter openers, lamps, and knives, though most were just butter knives. It was almost funny to look upon, if one hadn't seen the terror down below. I helped her into an overstuffed leather chair, careful not to touch any of the strings. She seemed to be coming around.

"Are you okay?"

She nodded. She reached forward and gave my hand a squeeze. I leaned over and hugged her tight. She hugged me back. That's when they entered. There were two of them, a man and a woman, bloody and wild eyed. They both had knives. I had nothing. They came at me at the same time. Spreading out, splitting the difference. The woman saw her in the chair. She lunged. I screamed. The man lunged too. Everything fell into chaos. The strings began to break and the various traps began to swing. A butter knife hit the man with no effect. His knife sliced my arm. She was wrestling with the woman on the floor, both of their hands on the handle of the knife. A heavy old fashioned desk lamp hit the side of my head. I snatched at it and began to swing with wild abandon. The man went down under my blows. I kept hitting until there was no possibility of him getting back up, then I went for the woman.

The woman was on top of her. I hit the woman with the lamp. I hit the woman again and again. The woman collapsed into a pile. I saw her eyes like the ocean. The knife sprang upward into my gut, her hands holding tightly to the handle were covered with my blood. She screamed.

"Get away from me."

I dropped the lamp and the knife pulled back. She said it again. Quieter than the first time.

"Get away from me."

The knife plunged into my belly again and pulled back. I staggered away, my hands clutching my wound, but I didn't make it far. I fell into one of the overstuffed chairs. The chair was facing the window. It was a beautiful day. White fluffy clouds racing through the sky. My gut hurt. Everything felt like it was on fire. She was back on her feet again. She came around and blocked my view. She looked tired. Her mouth was stuck in a hard line. She stared down at me. Her eyes were the same color as the lake. Everything hurt. The need was still there. I could feel the words on my lips. The words that I had to say. This was my chance. This might be my only chance. All I had to do was gather my strength. All I had to do was say it.

The knife was still in her hand. The blade was still crimson with my blood. I licked my lips and looked at her. I tried to force it out, but everything hurt. The knife moved forward. That's when I woke up. I don't know, a bit too much on the fucking nose for my tastes.

A Public Service Announcement

Please remember that it is against the law to smoke within ten feet of an entrance, exit, accessibility ramp, window that opens, and/or air intake vent. Please understand that this law is not in effect to protect you from the negative consequences of puffing away on your cancer sticks. We could really not give a shit over what method you choose to use to hasten your inevitable march towards death. Nor is this in any way meant to protect your fellow hyper-intelligent primates from the so-called dangers of inhaling secondhand smoke. Despite all of their pointed fake coughing, we find such worries well beneath the real concerns of the government.

These laws are in place to protect against gnome attacks. Yes, that's right. Gnome attacks. Did you know that gnome attacks are the 1,171,195th leading cause of death in the United States and that on average one person dies of gnome attacks every 11.62 years? While most of us prefer to imagine gnomes as those whimsical pointy hatted figurines lovingly placed in our grandmama's garden, in truth gnomes are red hatted bearded thugs who are willing to kill with little to no provocation. Thirsting for blood, gangs of gnomes run rampant throughout our cities, hunting for the unwary, waiting for the stupid to let their guard down. Do you know how many injuries are caused by gnomes? Zero. Gnomes are not playing. They are not interested in your valuables. No, gnomes are just interested in defecating on your corpse.

Smoking laws are in place to help keep the public spaces where we are at our most vulnerable safe from the gnome scourge. Gnomes are well known heavy smokers, never being far from their menacingly long pipes filled to the brim with a wide assortment of flavored tobaccos. Is that rich aroma the smell of Jan from accounting's smooth filterless Virginia Slim, or is it the pungent burning odor of dried dandelions and human hair emanating from a vile gnome calabash pipe with meerschaum bowl? There is no way to tell. Why take such a horrible risk? These laws are in place to protect you.

Remember, if you see a gnome, don't bother reporting it, because you're already dead.

Debate

Danny Cheswick - February 27 at 9:08 PM
Wow crazy, all the angry political rants I've been reading on
Facebook have totally changed America. I'm mean sure, here I
was thinking I was going to have to spend a whole bunch of time
actually doing stuff; you know, like writing a whole bunch of
letters, forming political groups with like minded individuals to
raise money for causes I believe in, giving money to election
campaigns (did you know you can give money to candidates not
living in your state, crazy as hell, but you can do it), and
volunteering my time; but nope, turns out just posting rants and
news articles has totally done the trick. Thank god. Here I was
worried that I might actually have to try to understand why the
other "side" feels the way it does, thus gaining empathy and a
better understanding that might better help me in my dealings in
the future, leading to more civil conversations that can actually
lead to changed minds, instead of just assuming that they are
dumb/evil. Thank goodness I can avoid that quagmire and
instead just scream at people in hopes of gaining accolades from
those that already agree with me. Welp, now that America is all

fixed, I'm going to have myself an extra beer. I probably don't need it, but I definitely deserve it.

Nick Greene - February 27 at 9:16 PM
Like I said to the last person (not that I believe your comment was directed towards me) who told me social media was not going to fix anything... they made an assumption that all I did was post my opinions on social media... they did not see all of the letters and phone calls and contributions... the fact that I am using social media as one of my tools does not indicate I am not utilizing other tools as well.

Danny Cheswick - February 27 at 9:57 PM
Fair enough, and good on you for the effort. However, using social media the way so many people are using it, which seems to be mostly just people angrily jerking themselves to the applause of those who agree with them, is just about useless, and in many ways harmful. What made me mad enough to post the above was seeing several people go after each other on here with the attitude of "if you don't meet my personal criteria related to my beliefs, you are a piece of shit." Change doesn't come from screaming into the air and demonizing the idiots on either side of the extremes (or just the people who disagree on a few things). It comes from going to those in the middle, having a civil conversation, and recognizing their issues, whatever they are, as legitimate. This isn't a game of scoring points on each other. This is the time to reach out with an open hand, not a fist.

Emily Fischer - February 27 at 10:34 PM
Sorry, I disagree. When the "other side" is about taking rights away from people, and recently advocating killing immigrants, there is no conversation that can take place. I will never understand why people think it's okay to take away someone's

civil rights based on their religion, skin color, or sexuality. It's not an understandable position.

Emily Fischer - February 27 at 10:35 PM
Also, you can't assume that people are solely ranting on FB. You're making assumptions.

Danny Cheswick - February 27 at 10:53 PM
Again... perhaps don't start with extremes. Assuming that everybody who voted for a candidate supports every crazy thing they do makes about as much sense as the candidate making the same assumption. There are most definitely people who voted for Trump who view the world as you describe it above, but there are also most definitely people who voted for Trump who do not. This second group is the important one, since they are the ones that might be swung, but the only way to do that is to find out and understand what issues made them vote the way they did. What's going on in their lives that made them willing to toss the dice that the crazy Cheetoh man might not have been as crazy as he seemed just for the chance at a little hope and change.

Danny Cheswick - February 27 at 10:54 PM
Also again, if you're doing other stuff, good on ya, move on, the post isn't about you, so there's nothing to get defensive about.

Emily Fischer - February 27 at 10:54 PM
I'm not talking about candidates. I'm talking about the individuals. People are actively advocating for the death of immigrants on FB. Stop making assumptions.

Danny Cheswick - February 27 at 11:12 PM
And they will not be convinced otherwise regardless of what we do, so better to concentrate on those who can be convinced in

159

order to in the future remove those from power who make devil's bargains with the vilest of the vile.

Emily Fischer - February 27 at 11:36 PM
I think that shaming people for what they post on FB because you don't think it will do any good is ridiculous. My FB is mine. I can post on it whatever I want, as can you. The difference is that you assume that people who post on FB are doing nothing else. And whether it changes anyone's mind or not is irrelevant. These people should be shamed back into the closet with these bullshit beliefs, and that's what happens when they get outed.

Jake Rollins - February 28 at 12:24 AM
Well duh. FB is a waste of time. Twitter, that is where the real political posts belong.

Nick Greene - February 28 at 4:47 AM
Agreed.

Nick Greene - February 28 at 4:47 AM
Lmao!!

Danny Cheswick - February 28 at 8:51 AM
Changing minds is important given that in the end it all comes down to votes. Even people hiding in shame closets still vote.

Emily Fischer - February 28 at 8:53 AM
Sure, they vote. But letting them think that their bigotry is okay is simply wrong. If we just "live and let live" with people like that, we allow those beliefs to flourish and spread.

Danny Cheswick - February 28 at 8:55 AM

Also again, probably not very helpful to focus on the folks on the extreme ends of the spectrum. They're pretty entrenched and get off on being ridiculed and ostracized since it allows them to, at least in their own minds, feel like victims.

Emily Fischer - February 28 at 8:59 AM
Those are the ones we have to focus on. Those are the ones who shoot unarmed Indian men in bars because they're brown. Pretending they don't exist gets people killed. You may be okay with that, but I'm not. One day one of those brown people who gets shot is going to be someone I know and care about. So I need to care about all of them now.

Danny Cheswick - February 28 at 9:05 AM
Shunning them is fine, it just doesn't make much sense to spend much time engaging them since it goes nowhere and it's what they want. Makes more sense to try to change the minds of the middle ground people, which means engaging them, listening to them, and trying to understand them. What's their wants and needs?

Emily Fischer - February 28 at 9:07 AM
So it's more productive to tell people that you claim to agree with that they shouldn't post on Facebook? Seriously? Do you think this post of yours has been productive? Do you think you've changed anyone's mind?

Danny Cheswick - February 28 at 9:29 AM
I don't know. Though it has created quite the discussion which has, so far, remained pretty civil. If nothing else, maybe some of the more conservative friends I have will look at your replies and start to better understand how scared a lot of people are, and maybe some of my more liberal friends will start thinking that maybe equating everyone who voted for Trump with being a

racist/misogynist/monster is not very helpful if the goal is to win the next election.

Emily Fischer - February 28 at 9:34 AM
Again, you keep making assumptions while accusing others of making assumptions. I don't think that everyone who voted for Trump is a racist/misogynist/monster, and have never said as much, most people I know have not, that's usually a straw man brought by "conservatives". The fact is that while not every Trump voter is a racist/misogynist/monster, they voted for one.

Your thinking that this is a productive conversation is rather silly. You are not changing anyone's mind. You are not creating thoughtful conversation. You're making accusations and assumptions that are incorrect and insulting, and telling people what they should and shouldn't do in their own space.

Danny Cheswick - February 28 at 9:42 AM
Yet this "unproductive" conversation has you just as involved in it as I am. Even if it's not changing minds, it is at least forcing the both of us to look at our own views in order to defend them, which is the next best thing.

Emily Fischer - February 28 at 9:45 AM
No. It's not. A pair of white people discussing whether or not it's ok to defend brown people is not the next best thing. It's mental masturbation, and completely useless. The fact that I've entertained it does not mean that I feel "involved". I simply have nothing better to do right this moment.

Danny Cheswick - February 28 at 9:59 AM
I believe the discussion is not about whether or not we should help defend people from racists, but whether or not Facebook is the best way to do so.

Nick Greene - February 28 at 10:00 AM
Lmao...Danny look at what you started. :)

Emily Fischer - February 28 at 10:14 AM
It's none of your business what I use my FB for though. You
don't get to decide what people should say on FB. And your
claims that people only rant on FB and do nothing else is you
yourself doing what you're accusing others of, making
assumptions. You don't know whether people have written
letters to lawmakers, or taken part in protests, or given to the
ACLU or Planned Parenthood. You're seeing that they posted
on FB and assuming that they've done nothing else, then
complained about it on FB. So since you posted a rant on FB
can I assume that all you ever do is rant on FB and don't actually
do anything to make real changes?

Danny Cheswick - February 28 at 10:22 AM
So it begins.....

Emily Fischer - February 28 at 10:28 AM
What begins? Hypocrisy? What are you doing in the real world,
outside of Facebook rants, to effect change? If you asked the
people that you're ranting about what they do I'm betting they'd
give you a bunch of information. Personally I write and call my
representatives. I donate to PP and the ACLU. I take part in
peaceful protests. And I engage in meaningful conversations
with people in my life.

Danny Cheswick - February 28 at 10:31 AM
The part where it shifts to personal attacks instead of discussion
on the topic.

Emily Fischer - February 28 at 10:37 AM

Where did I personally attack you? I asked you what you do outside of Facebook since you're ranting on Facebook accusing others of just ranting on Facebook. What of the above is an attack?

Emily Fischer - February 28 at 11:46 AM
I'm still waiting to find out where I personally attacked you? I'm confused. I've invited you into my home and you've partaken of my hospitality, food, and beer, and now you're claiming that I've attacked you but refuse to tell me how. Please explain. I've simply asked you a question about something you've been accusing others of.

Emily Fischer - February 28 at 11:56 AM
So next time someone invites you to an event at my home you'll first need to either apologize for making baseless accusations, or explain how I've attacked you so that I may apologize.

Danny Cheswick - February 28 at 1:03 PM
I was on a plane.

Emily Fischer - February 28 at 1:14 PM
So?

Danny Cheswick - February 28 at 1:36 PM
When debate reaches a stalemate, switch tactics by going to question the reliability of the poster. A good way to do this is to imply they are a hypocrite. For added effect, list off your own credentials and demand them in return. This tactic has two major benefits in that it puts the other side on the defensive and it shifts focus away from the primary topic of debate. It in effect creates a perfect chance to exit a topic with a feeling of superiority. If the poster offers credentials, you, in offering your own credentials first, have set yourself up as judge of whether or

not the poster's credentials count. It in essence becomes a who is a better person fight. If the poster refuses to list said credentials, then the claim of hypocrite can be reaffirmed and debate shut down. Either way, it is no longer about the original topic.

Emily Fischer - February 28 at 1:39 PM
Not at all. You are actually ranting on Facebook about people ranting on Facebook. I'm asking you what you do outside of Facebook, which you claim the people you're ranting do not do. That is not an implication of hypocrisy, that is the definition of it. You have yet to answer my question, instead deflecting by claiming that I'm personally attacking you, which I am not doing. I am discussing your statements, which is what you claim to want to do.

Danny Cheswick - February 28 at 1:42 PM
However, a clever poster can set up a joke via their initial post. This is best done using a logical paradox, such as putting a claim that Facebook is a terrible way to convey meaningful change in the world on Facebook. This creates an interesting conflict in that the more vigorously somebody disagrees with the assertion, the more it proves the point.

Danny Cheswick - February 28 at 1:49 PM
Welp, onto another plane for me.

Emily Fischer - February 28 at 1:50 PM
Perhaps someone clever could do that without just coming off as being douchey.

Nick Greene - February 28 at 5:09 PM
Lmao!!

They Should've Told You At The Door

Jiggling It

It was intermission, so I went to take a piss just like every other jackass in the Moda Center. We were all there to see the Cirque show Crystal, which wasn't very good, but I digress. Anyways, it took forever to get up to a urinal. Damn place ought to install a trough. Providence Park installed troughs, and the bathroom lines are much quicker now. Probably saves water too. Either way, I finally got up to a urinal and got ready to do my business when I noticed the guy next to me acting funny.

Now I want to put it straight front and center that I'm most definitely not the kind of guy who looks at other people's dicks in the bathroom. Hell no, I'm a keep your eyes on your own business kind of guy. But that being said, you know, it's hard not to notice things through your peripherals, especially if it seems a little off. Now again, I want to re-emphasize that I wasn't trying to look at some random guy's dick, though I must admit that I did catch just the briefest flash of skin when I noticed what it kind of looked like the bastard was doing.

You ever catch something out of the corner of your eye that doesn't look right, but you can't focus on it because it's just not the place to go gaping away to ascertain the truth? That's the kind of situation I was in because I'm pretty sure the guy next to me was jerking it. It's all about the motion. You know what I mean? When you're jiggling it, you're doing more of an up and down motion. Jerking it is more of a tug. It's a completely different movement. It's something that catches the eye because you know exactly what it is, but sure as hell don't expect to notice the guy next to you doing it in a public restroom.

I don't know. Maybe that's just the way the guy jiggles it. But he did it for a good thirty seconds, which seems like a pretty long jiggle to me. It's not like I could glance over for a good look. What was I supposed to do? Just stare at him? Maybe yell out that the perv next to me was cranking it? There was no way to be sure. It didn't help any that the guy was an Indian fella, you know, from India. Of course, the first thing that pops in my head is whether or not I'm convinced he's cranking it just because he's a minority. You know, implicit bias and all that shit. He's not like me, so therefore he must be some kind of deviant. But god, it was like thirty seconds. Maybe he was doing it, and I was giving him the benefit of the doubt just because he was a minority. Isn't that just as bad? Christ, I don't know.

Whatever the hell was going on, the fucker finally put it away and moved on. I'm not sure, but I'm pretty sure he was jerking it. You know, not like he was trying to get off or anything, just a couple of pulls for a little boost. Just a nice little shot of dopamine to get through the second half. I'll tell you one thing though, whatever the fucker was doing, he didn't flush. Bastard.

Totality

The sky begins to darken. Forty people stand in the yard, staring upward at the slowly shrinking sliver of the sun through tinted celluloid encased in cheap cardboard frames. Some are staring at the ground, gazing wonderingly at the ghostly shadows rippling across grass and blankets. The chickens, only moments before pecking contentedly for bugs, file dutifully into their henhouse. Planes crisscross the world above. Hot air balloons climb higher into the sky. Without the glasses it is impossible to see, nothing but a boiling point of light, but behind their shade churns a change waited for with baited breath.

She stands behind him, only a couple paces away. At times he looks back, gazing with the length of a man who knows he cannot be seen. Once she catches him, lifting her glasses to look at the world around her. Their eyes meet, she gives him a smile and then goes back to gazing at the spectacle above. What does it mean? It has been this way the entire weekend. He had sat next to her for most of the prior evening, listening to her flit from one story to the next, nodding his head, unsure what to say.

"I was pretty drunk, so my friend was trying to help me get my seatbelt on, and I don't know why I said it, but I just blurted out, hey, I've sucked tens of dicks, I got this."

Everyone laughed. The conversation moved around the circle. It was easier when others talked. He could throw in the occasional barb, catch a few chuckles, watch from the corner of his eye to see if she was entertained. She seemed entertained. It's been so long. More than a year. He isn't sure if he still has in him the knowledge that is needed. Not of the end, no, that is like riding a bike. The beginning. The conversations. The signs. She tucked a lock of hair behind her ear once when he spoke. A smooth leg reached out with deliberate precision and gave his foot, thrust upward by the cross of his legs, a gentle tap, the contact lasting slightly longer than it should have. Was it a hint of a smile that played across her lips, or just his imagination? He forced himself forward, establishing a back and forth. He had been able to do it once. He should be able to do it again. The tenuous connection made. Ten minutes. Twenty. Thirty before it was broken. Exhausting. Doubts. Why did he have so many doubts?

The other one stands next to her. He stands tall, a smile upon his face and a clever quip upon his lips, too quiet for others to hear. She smiles. What are they? Once they had been lovers, or at least that is what the rumors claim. The evening before, as the growing twilight surrendered the last vestiges of the daytime bright, they both disappeared from his view at the same time. The disappearance made him sick to his stomach. The bitter bile of jealousy, disappointment, and the knowledge of oneself playing the fool. His head moved from side to side, searching the growing dark for any sign, not daring to rise from his chair, fearing that others might realize the source of his agitation. It had all been imaginary. Nothing but the delusions of a lonely man no longer happy with his current state.

Perhaps, or maybe it was his fault. What signs had he given back? How closely had he played his own cards? She was only human, same as him, slave to lusts of the flesh. How often had he himself, back when such things still came naturally, given up on the hope in lieu of the certainty. It was his fault. He was an idiot. Out of practice. Cursed to wander the world in complete isolation. Perhaps not. It could have all just been his imagination. He did not know which could be worse, being a coward or a fool.

In the end he had risen and walked to the front of the house, his anxiety no longer able to be contained by a body at rest. The other one was there, standing and talking with a knot of people. He joined the circle for a bit and then split off to return to his place of rest. She was sitting there when he returned. She looked just as she had when she had seemingly disappeared. Her makeup unsmudged. Not a hair out of place. He talked with her for a bit, and then she said goodnight and slipped off to her tent.

The last sliver of the sun disappears behind the orb. The glasses fall away. The sunset surrounds them on every horizon. People scream. People howl. Some clap and hoot for the invisible hands which long ago set the intricate gears of astronomy turning. One woman in her mid-forties dances in place like an excited four year old on Christmas morning. Cameras and phones click, trying and failing to capture the moment. It starts deep down in his belly, the storehouse of primal urges and instinct. It rises upward, setting all of him a quiver with its energy. He can feel it pouring out of him, emitting from his eyes, mouth, and the tips of each of his fingers. People are laughing with tears streaming down their cheeks. The entire world is cut free, its master's power deflected, turned away into the never ending cosmos. They are alive. They are living beings on a tiny ball surrounded by nothing. What do they have to be afraid of?

She stands behind him only a couple of paces back. The other one is pointing, his finger and arm sweeping across the orange hues of the horizon. He closes the space in an instant, a few quick steps and then she is in his arms. No more wondering. No more worrying. They are so small and it is all so vast. She does not pull back. She does not try to escape. His lips meet hers and for a moment she melts in his arms, her hands coming up to rest on his cheeks. He can feel them rising up into the air, upward into the darkened sky, gravity no longer an issue.

The sun begins to peek out, just beads along the cratered edge. Her fingers curl on the side of his face and come down with a terrible tearing, drawing lines of pain to mark their path. She pushes him away, and for a moment he holds on, desperate not to sink, instinctively tightening his grip against the fall, but then a stronger arm intervenes. They break apart, and he can see fear and shock in her eyes. Somebody shouts something unheard. The other one's fist meets his face. He falls backwards, his nose gushing blood, back down to the earth below.

The herd is milling about, confused, the source of ecstasy forgotten as they surround the distraction, unsure what to do. Only he sees it. Only he gazes up in wonder at the beauty above. The other one is standing over him, one of many faces. People are shouting. People are yelling. Somebody reaches out with a foot and kicks him in the side. He wills the heavens to grind to a halt. He prays to stay suspended in the strange shadowy world without sin. The beads of light grow and with a flash bloom into a blazing glory. The bright rays dig their way into his eyes. It hurts, but he refuses to close them. Refuses to break the last tenuous connection. It is beautiful. It is just so very beautiful, and he dare not look away.

It's Getting Crowded In Here

They pack around you, each vying for attention. It might be easier if they queued up or something, but they won't. You know they won't. It doesn't work that way. It never works that way. They all have their needs. Their need to be seen. Their need to be understood. Their need to be remembered. Laughter. Tears. Joy. Embarrassment. Anger. Hatred. Shame. Despair. All just as fresh as the day they were bottled and put away. You can taste them on your lips. You can see them before your eyes. Every sound and smell tucked away. No detail too trivial. It's all there. All waiting expectantly for the dam to break, giving way to the onrush of it all. Drowning you below the waves of the crowd. You can feel them. Watching. Waiting. Ready to pour forth. You don't want them to. You want them to go away, but that's not how it works either. You know this. It will never be the way it should be. You will never taste the sweet draught of forgetfulness. The flavor of each vintage will never waver. Nothing will fade. Nothing will disappear into the depths. It all floats on the surface, so much flotsam, crashing together and fighting to rise to the top. Was it yesterday or five years ago?

It's hard to tell. It's hard to tell when everything feels the same. They're all the same. People that is. The same faces and the same stories. All bundled together in a ball of needs and wants. The need to survive. The need to be recognized. The need to be remembered. The same wants and needs, just variations in the same story told over and over again. Formulaic. It's all too much. They all blur together, but the edges stay sharp. Your heart races. Your back hurts. You can barely look down with the pain. Eating is a chore, shoveling sustenance into a roiling void, expelling endless piles of waste. You don't sleep. It's hard to think. What's the point? What's the point of any of it when it is all just the same. Change, you have to have change. Something to mark the years. Something to use to differentiate. It couldn't have been yesterday. It's in the old apartment. The one you lived in so long ago. It's an old one. Just disguised as recent, but it doesn't feel that way. No, it feels like it is right there in front of you. Not even a layer of dust to show the passage of time. The world rots away around you, but nothing rots within. Anguish. Oh dear god the anguish. Why does it have to be here? Why can't it fade away? It's nothing. Nothing more than anyone of the identical faces must face. It's selfish to think otherwise. You're not special. You're not unique. You're just another face in the crowd. No. There is more. The memories themselves are not unique, not even all that terrible in the grand scheme of things, but they are there. Imprinted. Saved in a format that will not degrade. They pile up. Higher and higher. All mixed together. No organization. No nothing. Just a massive pile of garbage with more thrown on every day. You do what you can to avoid adding to the pile, but it just adds more. It's not all bad. There are good things. It's not that you're smarter. It's just that you have more variables to include. Not worth it. It's definitely not worth it. Despair. Regret. Lost chances. Sacrificed to avoid adding to the pile. Damn that pile. Damn it to hell. Panic. Fear. Anxiety. Depression. Nothing

174

feels right. You can't sit still. Your mind refuses to stop turning. You lay in bed awake at night. Watching old movies in your head. None of your clothes feel comfortable. Nowhere that you rest brings relief. Your entire body feels uncomfortable. A foreign thing about to burst like a piece of rotten fruit. You want it all swept out. You want to feel clean. Unencumbered. Dreams. Just add them in with all the rest. Did that really happen or was it just an illusion? A fault in an otherwise perfect system. What is true and what is false? A whole world seen at a single angle. Incomplete views. Incomplete saves. You just want it all to stop. You just want it to all fade away. Hundreds of voices turn to thousands. Thousands turn to millions. How much can one mind hold? How can it all fit? Organized. It needs to be organized. Filed away. Older. You're older now. That one was from when you were younger. When did you get older? You don't feel any different. You feel exactly the same. Everyone else is moving, but you're standing still. Nothing changes. You refuse to let it change. You're frightened. Scared of the change and what it means. Time to add more to the pile. More jetsam amongst the bobbing waves. For fuck sakes. You're only thirty-four. If it feels this way at thirty-four, how is it going to feel when you're fifty? Seventy-five? They're all yelling. Screaming for attention. A sea of faces. Dragging you down. Down. Down. Suffocating you. Tighter. Tighter. Shut up you want to yell. Shut the fuck up all of you. It won't do any good. They're not there. They don't really exist. It's just you. That is all it is. It doesn't matter though. It doesn't matter what you know. It won't change the simple fact. It's getting crowded in here.

We Hope To See Such Heights Again

What is contentment? Contentment is a carpeted bathroom in a house that none of us will likely ever set foot in again, the memories too strong even if given the opportunity. The carpet was welcome given that it was a cold bathroom when we were children, rarely warm in any season except summer. To counter this cold, a wall heater was installed right next to the toilet. Contentment is sitting in a cold bathroom, feet buried in shag carpet, one side freezing while the other nearly burns. Just one more piece of wonder in a world of magic we will never forget.

If we got up early enough, we could have breakfast with Grandad. We just had to be okay with the silence. Grandad always got up first. Despite his size he'd slip quiet as a mouse down the hall to the kitchen. If one of us didn't get up and follow he'd eat alone. A simple breakfast of eggs and burnt toast. If any of us abandoned the warm solitude of our beds, we'd be greeted with little beyond a good morning and a query of whether or not we would like him to make enough for two. It was not always an easy decision. The eggs were cooked sunny side up, runny, even in the whites. There was rarely more than one of us that would get up early enough to eat breakfast in silence with Grandad. When breakfast was finished, he'd put his dishes in the dishwasher, pull on his coat, and put his cap upon his head, slightly crooked as it always was, all without a word. Off he would go into the first rays of light, the bells on the door jingling as he closed it. He would not return until evening, gone to the ranch spread across the country around Fossil, from the heights of the mountains to the river in its deep cleft. We rarely saw any of it. It was a separate world from that of the house. A place apart.

We would get up one by one, all three of us. We would gather quietly in the kitchen where we would pour a mixture of sugar filled cereals into low sided plastic green bowls, a bounty denied us when we were at home. Grammie worried less about such things. In fact she promoted them. One of our first stops when arriving in Fossil would always be the mercantile, where we were each allowed to pick the box of our choice. Coco Puffs. Cookie Crisp. Cinnamon Toast Crunch. Honey Grahams. No child would have been foolish enough to select Kix or Cheerios. With our bounty in hand we would slip to the living room to watch television, always making sure to keep the volume low. Grammie never rose before eight, and it was the unwritten rule not to disturb her. She was retired, and retired people get to choose when they rise.

The TV sat in the corner of the room, contained by a cabinet with folding doors and drawers full of movies both purchased and recorded. The TV had a remote, still a rarity in those days, and one of the first VCRs we had ever laid eyes on, a big heavy box of silver plastic which greedily sucked in the tapes offered to it. It would grind and make strange sounds, and the tracking dial always had to be fussed with to clear the screen, but there would be what we wanted to watch when we wanted to watch it. A miracle in our time.

Grammie would rise promptly at eight, but nobody would disturb her. She would come down the hall to the kitchen in a bathrobe as red as a firetruck, saying not a word. She would pour herself a cup of coffee and drink it slowly, savoring the first morning sips, nibbling on toast with cinnamon spread thickly over a quarter inch of margarine. If any of us ventured in she would say good morning and make sure we had gotten something to eat. The ritual complete, she would return to her bedroom to change, emerging in pants and blouse of bright colors, transformed into a beaming sun ready to bring radiance to the day.

Much as we almost never saw the ranch where Grandad toiled, the bedroom he and Grammie shared was just as rarely visited. At the end of the hall it sat with its door mostly closed. Inside was the bed where they slept at night, surrounded by large ornate dressers of painted wood and one wall dominated by a matching vanity with mirror and stool. The bedroom had its own bathroom which we only visited in times of greatest need, but the image of which was firmly embedded in all of our minds. Toilet, sink, and tub, all were Pepto Bismol pink. The main bathroom, the one we always used, was the pink bathroom's twin, only with the color scheme switched to mint green. Grammie always said she hated the color schemes of her bathrooms, but no attempt was ever made to change them. The mint green bathroom had carpet in it. All of the house had carpet in it. Even the kitchen. The living room carpet was the greatest of all, shag with thick multicolored threads of green, black, and blue. Grammie would rake it from time to time.

Grammie getting dressed was the signal for us to get dressed as well. We were children, and it was expected that we play all morning, but that was no reason to spend the day in our pajamas. It was a place with no shortage of things to do. The entirety of the house was filled with drawers and cupboards, all overfilling with a collected bounty purchased with the intent of making a child smile. Mat towns and matchbox cars, plastic cowboys and indians, puzzle books and old board games. We would play with all of them, a movie on TV always in the background. Such was the world that Grammie created. With her own hands she made buildings of yarn and plastic grids. A farmhouse, barn, post office, church, covered bridge, city hall, school, and more. An entire town made just for us. In the garage was an electric train, moving in its never ending circle. Outside, in a great cauldron, were Tonka trucks and older, some that had been played with when Grandad was a child.

Out of it all, the most sought for was the computer. The first one we could remember in somebody's home. It sat in a small open room between the living room and the hallway, surrounded by stacks of video games in their colorful boxes. Grammie loved gadgets. Where others could spend hours wandering through aisles of clothes, she could do the same in electronics and office supply stores. The house was filled with firsts, amongst them a fax and a small copy machine, but there were smaller ones as well. Handheld poker and blackjack games, an electric coin sorter, small devices meant to suck up lint, and even a small slot machine. However, the computer reigned over all. We were each allowed an hour, though at times we got more. Together solving ancient riddles, delivering pizzas, and countless other adventures too numerous to mention. Grammie herself was not immune, though her time on the machine was mostly spent playing mahjong solitaire.

Despite its pull, the computer was not allowed to dominate our lives. There was too much to do. We played amongst the shag of the living room carpet, surrounded by the past and present, staring through floor to ceiling windows from the red brick house on the hill to the town below. Grammie always hated those windows and often joked that she wished we would play football near them in hopes that one might be smashed. However, none of us were ever that into sports. The furniture of

the house was both old and new, the latter collected from both
sides of family members long gone. The couch, a reupholstered
monstrosity of wood, held the distinction of being in an old
photograph of Grammie as a baby. The house itself was modern,
a single story brick structure built on a slab of concrete in the
joyous days after the end of the war. Diplomas and awards hung
on faux wood paneled walls to honor relatives living and dead,
scattered amongst paintings, prints, and other various wall
hangings.

There were always dogs in the house. The only other pet
was a goldfish of prodigious size. In the early days there were
mostly two dogs. An old retired border collie named Pattie and a
small dog with a round body and thick black curly hair named
Tar. There were other dogs as well, but they spent their days
with Grandad, and so were little seen except in the morning and
evening. Pattie mostly spent her time sleeping under Grandad's
desk in the garage, but Tar would spend her day wandering the
house, nose to the ground, searching for crumbs. A vacuum
cleaner on legs. These two would pass as all eventually do, but
were replaced by Katie, a border collie who became Grammie's
constant companion. A loving dog of strong intelligence who
Grammie swore was always trying to talk, if only she could get
her mouth to make the correct shapes to form words. Katie
would play, delighting in our company as much as Grammie, but
eventually her patience would fail, and she would slink off
behind the couch to hide.

Lunch was a casual affair, mostly prepared from a box.
Grammie was many things, but a great cook was not one of
them. Hot dogs, Spaghetti-O's, and Velveeta Shells and Cheese.
Sometimes soup and grilled cheese. Pepsi was always the drink
of choice, though Grammie always made us wash off the top of
the can in the sink. Lunch was eaten on trays in the living room,
so that movies could be enjoyed with the dogs combing hungrily
beneath our feet. Often, a piece of food would drop on purpose.

Though Grammie surely noticed, she never said a thing. Sometimes we would be taken down into the town to Chica's, the only restaurant for miles. Once a grocery store, we would sit and mention what used to be where we sat. We're sitting where the tomatoes used to be, and over there was the meat counter. People would come up and say hello and Grammie would introduce us, expecting each of us to appear as gentlemen to the world.

Afternoons would be for more play, the occasional chores, and at times a grand adventure. The most common was going to the fossil beds behind the high school where one was allowed to dig up their own fossils to keep. Though beasts of the past were never found, leaves and ferns were in abundance. Some larger pieces would be taken back home where they could be cracked by hammers, separating layers to show the treasures within. When we were hungry we snacked from the bowl of popcorn that inevitably always appeared. Breakfast cereal was another option for a midday snack, and we were always welcome to have another Pepsi. Often times we would sit with Grammie in the big dining room, the one only used for holiday dinners, and work on penny collections and listen to stories about a world now gone, both within her own memory and before.

Grandad always came home around six. He'd come in the house and say hello before drifting back into silence. Grammie would make dinner and we would eat it again on the trays in the living room. Grandad would sit in a straight backed chair with no footstool and watch sports on the television. When he fell asleep as he always did we would try to change it, but he would jerk awake and change it back. Heavy curtains would be pulled over the floor to ceiling windows and the house would drift to silence. We would play quietly amongst the shag, Grandad snoring softly and Grammie doing needlepoint in her chair next to the fire. Eventually bedtime would come, though always a little later than was expected when we were at home. Grandad would be awakened so we could each give him a hug goodnight, and dutifully we would file down the hallway to our room.

Time would be given to use the bathroom and brush our teeth, before Grammie would come back to tuck us in goodnight. We rarely showered while we were there, being still young enough to play without producing any stink, but at times Grammie would take a hot washcloth to our faces and arms. The bedroom we shared had two matching twin beds on either wall. Between sat an old dresser with small lamps on both ends, small flowers on them matching the design of the comforters. The youngest of us slept on a folding mattress on the floor, covered by well worn *Peanuts* sheets and thick blankets. Grammie would tuck us in tightly and then hit play on a tape player. The stories of James Herriott, *Chitty Chitty Bang Bang*, and many more would lull us off to sleep. Old friends which we listened to one side at a time. We would say our good nights and she would turn out the lights and shut the door. Sleep would come, with smiles upon our lips.

Memories are stones in the river of time. They remain while we continue on. All things pass. Sometimes I drive through the town and look up at the red brick house on the hill, and wonder if I shall ever reach such heights again.

They Should've Told You At The Door

A Letter To Neal deGrasse Tyson

Dear Neal deGrasse Tyson,

Thank you for your recent letter letting us know that the positions of the stars during the penultimate ship sinking scene of our movie Titanic were in totally the wrong positions for the historically accurate date of April 14, 1912.

While you are most definitely correct in your assertion that the stars are in the wrong locations, we as the creators of this film must ask, what the hell is wrong with you? We made a film that lots of people enjoyed, but somehow you think we, and the vast majority of people watching it, give a shit about where the stupid stars are.

Now we're not saying that star position isn't important. For instance, if we're talking about launching rockets or doing an astrophysics experiment, we better damn well know the right positions of the stars. However, we're not doing those things. What we're doing is telling a kind of stupid story about a budding romance between a spoiled rich girl and an effeminate leading man, who may or may not really be a woman (at least according to our favorite fan theory). The correct positioning of the stars really adds nothing to the story.

To be frank, the fact that you watched our (possibly lesbian) romantic movie and felt the need to send us a letter regarding the nitty gritty of star positions really says more about you then it does us. We would suggest taking a deep breath, maybe going for a run or something, and then coming back to enjoy our stupid movie for what it is. We wish you the best.

With love and respect,
James Cameron and Friends

Strategic Retreat

You can feel the warmth of his body close to yours, the heat of his breath on the back of your neck. His long fingers move through your hair, caressing the individual strands, selecting carefully the ones to pull tight between his ring and index digits. You stare at the wall in front of you in silence, staring at old black and white photos framed and covered in dust. It's a gentle tug, a soft reminder of his presence before the soft schick of the scissors signals the release. The hair falls down upon the barber cloth, sliding to join its fellows in your lap, pushing a few further to the front to the final drop to the floor below.

An old man sits in one of the three plastic chairs which line the wall beneath the glass window. He reads a *Sports Illustrated* and glances from time to time impatiently at the TV playing ESPN on mute. You ignore him as he ignores you. In this tight little world there is just the barber, and it is your turn in the chair. The hands and scissors move quick and sure, blending it all together, their knowledge of your scalp's terrain born of years of monthly explorations. Around the sides, circling the ears, deft in their motions. He moves to the left and right. He backs away and leans back in. The scissors move seemingly at random. A scattered attack here and then there, catching the last bits of work still to be done. He takes a comb from its jar of blue liquid, wets it in the sink, and then runs it through your hair, humming happily to himself before the big reveal. The old man has abandoned his magazine, eying you with anticipation.

The chair spins and then there you are, a reflected vision in the big mirror of the man that you've always been, no longer hidden away beneath the unkempt thatch upon your head. The barber fusses with his comb in last minute touch ups, until with a self-satisfied sigh he steps back to let you fully gaze upon the glory of his creation. You stare at yourself, knowing that the image smiling back at you will be the best that you'll look all month. A handcrafted treasure sculpted by the master in less than twenty minutes. You're not a bad looking man. There's a little gray at your temples and the alleyways are growing deeper and wider, but you're still providing a good canvas for his work.

The barber holds aloft a mirror and angles it this way and that to give you a look at the full three hundred and sixty degrees of his masterpiece. He waits with bated breath. The old man rises slightly from his chair. You study yourself carefully, taking it all in. You run your hands through your hair, mussing the carefully laid structure, letting it fall to see how it lays. Something doesn't feel quite right. You can't put your finger on it, but there is definitely a difference from times before. The barber is growing anxious. You're taking too long. He asks politely how it looks. You stare into the mirror. Fine you say. It looks just fine.

The barber's face splits into a wide smile. The old man rises and grunts. The barber brandishes his small hand broom and sweeps away the sacrificed ends onto the floor, brushing your neck with abandon. Off comes the cape. Off comes the paper around your neck. You rise and dig through your wallet. Before you can even hand over the twenty dollar bill the old man is already filling your seat. You look the barber in the eye, tell him to keep the change, and with a round of farewells head out the door. It's cold outside. A brisk fall morning on the downward rush towards afternoon. You wait until you're back in your car around the corner before you run your fingers through your hair again. Something is definitely wrong.

You check again at the stoplight. The hair is soft to the touch. The car behind you honks when the light turns green. You tell yourself to stop. You're just acting crazy. You've been going to the same barber for years. He always does a good job. When you get home you go up to the bathroom. You stare at yourself in the mirror. You look good. It's a good haircut. You run your hands through your hair again and again. Feeling. Probing. Searching. It's thicker in the back than it is in the front, but that's nothing new. You see a flash of scalp in the front as your hands pass by.

It's then that you know. You know exactly what it is. He's left the hair in the front longer. That's why it looks so good. He's left more to help camouflage the slow retreat. More to help cover that which has been lost by nature's cruel joke upon your sex. The realization puts a hard knot in your guts. Another sign of your impending doom. He never said a word about it. He never gave a single hint to reveal the ruse. He just did it. He just slipped it in with the grace of an artist. You cannot blame him. His job is to make you feel good. His job is to make you smile at yourself in the mirror. But at what cost? It's a slow retreat. Imperceptible to the naked eye, but you know that it is happening every day. Occasionally you'll be sitting, reading a book, and you'll find a hair. Sometimes in the shower, after massaging in the shampoo. When you clean the lint trap. Everybody loses hair, but not everyone feels the deep seated sadness of those who know it's just a matter of time.

You stare at yourself. You do look good, but what will you look like tomorrow? How long can you continue lying to yourself? How far can you let the delusion go? Today it's just longer in the front, but how long until it becomes the careful coifing of ever lengthening survivors? How long until they pass as well, replaced by their brethren along the sides? Is this how it happens? Is this why you see such men? Proud old lions with comb overs, smiling confidently with a secret more obvious to the rest of the world than it is to themselves. Lions who are laughed at behind their backs, the full sadness of it all hidden from them by the gradual pace of nature and the helping loving hands of an artist. Delusional to the point of convincing themselves that this is the way it's always been. That nothing has changed. That Delilah hasn't come and stolen it all away.

No. You go to the closet and find the small vinyl bag. You go into the bathroom and pull out its contents. You plug it in. You turn it on. It buzzes in your hand. You stare at yourself in the mirror as the hair falls. Short and long the strands plummet downward, revealing to the world that which is hidden underneath. You will not fall into such a fate. You will not be some hapless pawn under the influence of unseen hands. No, if you must fall then you will jump, arms outstretched, ready to immerse yourself in the world as it is.

Darkness

The nights always feel the worst, that's always when you feel
the most alone. At the end of the evening you prepare yourself
for the darkness that comes when you turn off the lights. You
don't think about it, you don't let it worry you, but then the
lights go out and all you can feel is that great emptiness growing
deep inside. You lay in the darkness and listen to the night
sounds as your home settles into the great depths of the dark and
you reach out hoping to find something there, but there is
nothing. Nothing but your own worries and anxieties
multiplying in the depths. You wait for the dreams to take you,
but they don't come. You lay in the darkness alone. They don't
understand. How can they? They lay next to those they love
and never give a thought about what it truly means to have them
there. When they stare down into the precipice their hand holds
the hand of another, and they take comfort. Cursed are we who
walk the world alone, surrounded only by the ghosts of what
might have been. Screaming silently into the void. Throwing
ourselves violently against our chains as we yell that no, they
will not take us, they will not entwine us, they will not drag us

down into the depths. Our defiance is all we have, but it is tainted, tainted by the knowledge that it cannot sustain us, and we know it is only a matter of time before we fall as all have before us and all who will come after. We wait for the light of day and the empty reasons to carry on, but we cannot lie to ourselves in the dark. We know truly who we are. We shriek in terror, but have nothing to cling to, no other souls amongst the flotsam of our lives. It is all nothing, and into this lack of anything we must stare alone. We fill our days with experiences, yet for what, for it all means nothing when the darkness comes. We flail blindly as we fall, stoic in our pain, quietly praying that our groping fingers find those of another before we hit the unseen ground below.

Cocky Monster

"Cocky Monster died."

We were all a little shocked, but overly not surprised. Maybe that's a little harsh, but let's just call it what it was. Cocky was a drug addict. He died of an overdose. One morning he didn't answer his phone and when people went looking for him at his house, boom, there he was, dead. You have to expect such things when someone does that kind of shit all the time. It's just the facts of life. If Icarus couldn't fly too close to the sun without getting burned, then what hope did Cocky have? None, that's what.

I don't know. Maybe that's being a little too indifferent, but what can you expect? Most of us hadn't seen him in years. He and most of the people he normally hung out with just kind of drifted away, started doing their own thing more, faded into memories of the good old days. Crazy bastards. What are you supposed to do? Leave a comment on a Facebook post and that's about it. No inquiries about what happened. No questions about the funeral. Hell, none of us had any plans to go. Why would we? Hadn't seen him in years. More memory than person, and hell, he was likely not the person he once was anyways. Best to leave things to those who still saw him regularly. Those who really gave a shit. The best any of us could do was sit and wonder if we were going to feel any pangs at all, waiting because that's what it felt like we ought to do. How long does one have to wait until they just accept the reality of the situation? One could feel bad about not feeling anything, but then they're just making it about them, not him. That doesn't seem right.

I wish I had started this differently. I could, but what's the point? It's the way a lot of people are going to chalk it up. Drug addict dies of drug overdose. No surprises. Short and simple. He deserved better than that. He was one of the nicest guys I ever met. Well actually, he wasn't really all that nice. In fact, a lot of times he could be a real son of a bitch, but by god, he was a loveable son of a bitch.

I don't know. Maybe it was his nonchalance about most things, though that isn't quite right either, given the number of times I saw him lose his temper. In the end I think it was his acceptance of the people around him. He could think you were the biggest chode in the world, and he'd tell you so too, the man had no filter on him, but even if he did he wouldn't hold it against you. As long as you accepted him as is, he did the same for you. Everybody was the same to him. He'd see you, smile, and ask how the hell you were doing. Even meant it most of the time. None of that pleasantries crap. If he didn't want to know, he wouldn't have asked. He'd even listen to you if you wanted him to, though he might just walk away when you were done. You don't find many people with that much honesty. It's something rare.

One of my favorite memories of Cocky was the couch burning. Ditch had an old couch, so she hauled it over to Cocky's house to light that mother up. A whole bunch of us went to watch. Made it a big production. An excuse to drink

194

beer in the middle of the week. Cocky of course made it bigger. He had a whole pile of shit he needed to burn so it all got added on. I'm pretty sure some of it didn't need to burn, but once a fire was going there was little reason to waste the opportunity. Well, given that it was a pretty big bonfire within the city limits I'm sure you can imagine what happened. It didn't take long for those big red trucks to come racing down to the field behind Cocky's house.

Cocky of course decided that he was the best one to take care of it. While the firefighters put out the bonfire he marched over to talk to the man in charge. He was of course a humorless bastard, the type that's gotten worn out by too much shit, which was probably the worst type to have to deal with Cocky as an emissary. Every single one of his statements was met by a sweet innocence so overwhelming that Cocky had him gagging in no time. Poor son of a bitch had no idea what he was up against.

"Why are you putting it out?"

"You can't have a fire this big."

"Well shit, how big of one can I have?"

"Three feet by three feet."

"Well, me and my friends are just combining each of our legal little fires into one big one."

It was pretty damn entertaining to watch. The guy in charge of course got mad. How could he not? So Cocky got mad too, matching each upward notch every step of the way. When the guy threatened to give Cocky a ticket he got into his truck, he had a big lifted truck, and started doing cookies around the perimeter of his property, screaming random obscenities and hanging one arm out the window to flip off friend and foe.

"Communist assholes! No fun here!"

The guy of course wrote Cocky a three hundred dollar ticket. Cocky didn't care. He just took the damn thing and laughed. You never saw a man in authority look so powerless. With a fcw last threats they left. The rest of us dispersed not long after. There was really no dealing with Cocky once he got like that.

I don't know. The guy definitely had his problems. There were definitely some demons somewhere in there. He was always drinking too much and I don't think I ever saw him not high on something. Most of us never bothered to ask what. It felt like none of our business. He was good people though. One of the best. You could probably tell the jackass you were fucking a goat and he'd just hand you a beer. Treat it the same as talking about the weather. It wouldn't be that he agreed with you or condoned such behavior, just that he saw it really as none of his business. The world could use more people like that.

Anyways, like I said, it wasn't that surprising. I thought it was the end of him when he wrecked his motorcycle a few years before, but he pulled through that alright. Didn't change him one bit. I guess it's not that he went that was shocking, just that he went so quietly. I always expected something more. You know, like a police shootout or something. Something that would pop up on the evening news. No luck though. No luck at all.

The Girl From Fargo

The flight to Fargo takes six hours counting the layover in Minneapolis. I'm on the same flight as my boss, but I don't sit next to him. This is by design. I never like sitting next to people that I know on flights. It's my time. My time to be alone, or at least as alone as one can be in a giant flying cigarette. Even if I didn't need the alone time I would avoid sitting next to my boss. I don't like him. Why is not important, at least in the context of this story. Better to stay focused on what's important. We don't want to be all fucking day about this.

The moment we land the cabin is filled with the jingles of starting phones and the chimes of incoming text messages. I don't turn on my phone. I'm proud of myself for not doing so. It makes me feel like I'm better than those around me. A sober man at the bar. It's silly to think so. I exit the plane with the rest. The air is warm. The grass is green. Fargo is not my home. I'm only visiting. Three days for work and then four days to drive around Lake Superior. Why Lake Superior? Why not? It's there. It's a place. It will add some more dots on a map that I keep for myself. A dot for every locale I've ever been. It's a goal with no consequences if I fail.

I'm not feeling all that well. Physically I'm fine. It started on the plane. Not the one I just got off, but the one that landed in Minneapolis. With my head pressed against the plastic of the fuselage it came to me. A perfectly intact memory that I'd rather just forget. Preserved. A mosquito in amber. An image with eyes like the ocean that fails to drift by but instead sticks front and center. It doesn't cause the panic it once did, but it's still an annoyance. A reminder. One begets another and they sail upwards in a swarm, overwhelming in their clarity. Five years. I'm getting old. Thirty-three is not old, but so little feels like it has changed. In certain ways I might as well still be sixteen. Stagnation.

I wait at the baggage claim. A co-worker of mine comes down the escalator and we make small talk. He is an older gentleman wearing slacks and a dress shirt. I'm wearing jeans and a t-shirt. We have little in common. The conversation jerks its way forward, falls silent once again, and then grows still. My boss comes down the escalator. He prattles about nothing. We stand and wait as the bags flow by. Most are black and blue, a never ending cycle of sameness, but a few are bright splashes of color and variety. I have to remind myself that I'm looking for a blue bag. I used to have a red bag, bright red, but a few months ago, during a trip to Winnipeg, the handle wouldn't drop back down. The problem had been solved by placing the handle against a concrete pillar and giving the bag a hard kick, snapping off the handle.

We claim our bags. Mine is one of the last ones as always. We go out to the short bus that takes us to the hotel. The zit covered driver fills the luggage hold to the top. One of the middle buttons of his rumpled shirt has come undone. The bus is full. I cram in next to a big man wearing a smiling cowboy hat. He looks like a stereotype. Wrangler jeans, belt buckle, and a pearl snap shirt with the shape of a snus can in the front pocket. He's so big that I can only get half my ass on the seat. Our legs are pressed together. It's a little too intimate for my tastes. The cowboy nods at me.

"You going to the conference too?"

I can't be impolite.

"Which one?"

"International Livestock Identification."

I shake my head.

"Wheat trade."

The cowboy looks up at the front of the bus and then back at me.

"Where you from?"

"Portland. You?"

"Calgary."

I try to split a warm smile, but it feels only half done.

"Oh yeah, I used to live up by there."

The cowboy gestures with his hand and corrects himself.

"Well, not really Calgary, a little north?"

"What, like around Red Deer?"

"Olds."

"University town."

"Yeah."

I give him a knowing nod.

"I used to live at Drumheller. Seven years ago. Worked for a feedlot by Acme."

"Highway 21?"

"Yeah."

I leave it at that. Who knows what kind of reputation the connection evokes, if any. Maybe it's just a name. The conversation comes to an end. Sure, I could've talked about how I grew up on a cattle ranch, but why? We never talk again. Over the next several days I see him walking around a couple of times amongst the sea of cowboy hats that make up half of the people filling the hotel's conference center and bar. The two groups flow around each other but never mix. The song "The Farmer And The Cowman" keeps playing through my head throughout my stay. You know, from *Oklahoma*. Maybe you don't. Maybe your grade school music teacher didn't make you watch televised musicals whenever they didn't feel like teaching.

Anyways, the bus grinds to a halt. I get out, grab my bag, and head inside quick to beat the crowd. I check-in. I see more coworkers in the lobby, ones I don't mind being around. We trade hellos and make plans to get dinner. I take my bags up to my room, take a shit, and head back down to the lobby. There's five of us all together, three around my own age and one in his fifties. We have to take two Ubers, which accounts for all of the Ubers in Fargo. We make it an unofficial race, which the car I'm in totally wins despite its less than impressive maintenance record. Every time it hits a bump the shocks grind. The pile of flesh driving claims he knows some shortcuts down some back alleys. He has the air of a socially awkward serial killer, the kind who can't understand why his hands keep getting covered in blood.

The restaurant seems out of place in Fargo, or at least out of place for what I would characterize as my stereotype of Fargo. It's fancy. The servers all wear white shirts. That's not the part that's out of place. Throughout the restaurant hang abstract art sculptures of various animals frozen mid-mutation into monsters. Across from our table one entire wall is covered in hundreds of bathroom floor tiles from a hundred different bathrooms with a few pieces of broken mirror randomly thrown in for ambience. The decor provides some conversation, but it quickly devolves into the two women in the group talking over each other, neither minding if anyone is really listening. A battle of wills to shift the focus. The older coworker goes quiet. He seems tired. I think he might be annoyed, but it might just be me projecting.

We finish our dinner and walk up the street to a bar which sits next to the railroad tracks through the center of town. Dilapidated is being polite. The interior is dark, but not dark enough to hide the grime. It's filled with mismatched chairs partially filled by drunks old and young at various stages of melting into their surroundings. We sit down and order a round of drinks. I order a canned beer. God knows when the last time they cleaned out their hoses. The fight for topical dominance begins again. I wander away and play Big Buck Hunter, my go to when I need a social break. I'm getting pretty good at it. The older coworker watches me and gestures at the machine when I return.

"You must be pretty good at that."

I can't tell if he's being serious or facetious.

"I play it a lot."

We order a second round of drinks. I check the time on my phone. Not having much else to do I open the Bumble app and start scrolling through women. It helps pass the time. Bumble is a dating app. Profiles are simple. Pictures and a short statement. If you like what you see, swipe right. If you don't swipe left. If they like you too it's a match. Ladies have to message first. If they don't in twenty-four hours the match is lost. I swipe right on the first ten pictures that pop up. I don't even bother to look at half of them. I've never done this before. I've never swiped outside of Portland. I don't know why. That's a lie. I feel a little embarrassed, but nobody pays any attention to what I'm doing.

We take the same two Ubers back to the hotel. I go up to my room, iron my nice clothes, and watch a movie. It's getting late. I set the alarm on my phone. Three matches. I look at the profiles. Two are cute, one not so much. I need to go to bed. I masturbate. Not to the Bumble pictures, that seems creepy, but to nudie pics I Google image search on my phone. I clean up and out go the lights. No sounds but the hum of the air conditioner. Flotsam and jetsam floats to the top, broken loose by the thought on the plane coming into land in Minneapolis. I think about the Bumble girls. Three matches in just a few hours. Not bad.

Three days of meetings. I won't bore you. God knows they bored the shit out of me. Lots of sitting on one's ass and listening to people speak about things you already know. After the first night of meetings, I go out to dinner with some farmers from Montana and then have some drinks with them at the hotel bar. Nice fellas. Easy going. Down to earth. The type that don't really have an angry bone in their bodies. I don't even think about the Bumble girls. Hell, it's not like I'm from here. I'm getting a little old for the whole one night stand thing. Been there done that. Besides, I doubt if I'm really charming enough to pull it off via text. I get out my phone to check the time. The notification is on the screen.

Amy has sent you one message.

One of the farmers asks me a question. I put my phone back in my pocket and answer with a joke. The table laughs. We have another round. I excuse myself to go use the bathroom. I lock myself in a stall and get back out my phone.

Hi there.

Her profile is fairly succinct. Nothing written, just pictures. She's thin. Most of her outfits are fairly conservative, though a couple show off her body. Blonde hair cut below her shoulders. In a couple, she wears a pair of glasses with thick black frames resting on a sharp nose. I'm not sure, but she looks a little cockeyed. One photo is her with an old man, probably her grandfather or something. A little bit of makeup, but not too much. None of the usual photos. No bathing suits, rock climbing, or whatever other bullshit seems to be in every profile. She's pretty. Attractive in a way you don't often see swiping through Bumble in Portland. No frills. No hipster bullshit. Nor does she have the bedazzled ass jeans that seem to be the big

thing everywhere that doesn't have a coast. I'm a little drunk.
I'm not sure how to answer. I'm not sure if I should answer. I
start and stop a couple of responses. The bathroom smells like
shit. Not a big surprise, what with it being a bathroom and all,
but it helps force my decision.

Hello. How are you doing this evening?

I go back out and buy another round. It's my turn. I try to
keep myself from checking my phone again and again. I don't
want to be rude to the others at the table. Never mind the fact
that obsessive compulsive is rarely an attractive trait. Three
minutes becomes the record. The constant looking does nothing
to help speed up the response. My phone finally beeps.

*I'm not too shabby! I'm currently at work. What are you up
to?*

Work? It's around ten in the evening? What the hell does
she do for work? The farmers are talking about tractors or
something. I politely feign interest and type back a response.

Just got back from dinner. I'm in town for a conference.

More waiting.

So you don't live here?

I feel guilty the moment I see it. Skeezy. What kind of guy
uses a dating site to pick up women in a town he's going to be
leaving soon. Before I can reply she sends an addendum.

Where do you live?

You know, maybe I'm thinking a little too much into this.
Who am I to make decisions for someone else? She's an adult.
Besides, she is pretty damn attractive, never mind the casual use
of the word shabby, one of my personal favorites. It doesn't hurt
any that the beer sloshing around in my belly is giving me a little
more balls than normal.

*I'm actually from Portland, Oregon. In town a couple
nights, then heading to Duluth.*

I hit send. It doesn't feel like enough. It feels like I should add something. You know, to at least make it sound like I'm a nice guy trying to get in her pants.

I'm sorry for the confusion.

There we go. Not the most eloquent, but it gets the job done. No reply. I finish my last beer and say my goodnights. No answer. Yep, that did it. Just another random guy on the road looking to get his dick wet. Nothing to see here. I go back to my room and get ready for bed, looking for excuses as I go. Is it really all that wrong? It's just another need. Just like taking a shit. Something you have to do. Yeah, but they don't always feel that way about it. Look at all the trouble you've gotten yourself in. You've told yourself that you're going to be less selfish. That you're going to quit using what happened five years ago as an excuse. Shit knows you've caused enough problems. Never mind the current poor girl at home. Strung along like a fish, but never reeled into the boat. Always brought in close, but then let back out. Forget about it. Just go to bed and forget about it. My phone dings.

No problem.

Hot damn, we're in business. I sit on the edge of the big king sized bed and try to think of something to say. I need to wait a little bit, but not too long. I don't want to seem overeager, but I don't want to seem uninterested. I can see her stretched out naked on the bed. I can feel my lips…...No, no, that's not what this is. It's just meeting somebody new. Taking a risk. That's right. Less thinking about sex, more thinking about meeting someone interesting. These trips can get boring. I know I have a problem letting my guard down enough to meet people. This is about improving myself as a person.

What do you do for work?

There we go. That's a good innocuous question. Just showing a little interest in someone besides myself. Getting to know them. It's not about sex, but if that's where it leads….

I'm a newspaper designer.

Okay, that's actually interesting. How many damn newspaper designers have I ever met? Zero, that's how many.

That's pretty cool. So you set up how all the articles, ads, and everything else goes together?

Jesus. That's pretty cool. What am I? Nineteen? Lame.

I don't do ads. That's a whole different department (the dark side). I design and lay out the news, write headlines, size photos, stuff like that. I just finished the front page of the Fargo Forum.

I like her, or at least as much as you can like someone from a few texts back and forth. She seems funny and down to earth, like someone I'd get along with. Hell, it would just be enjoyable spending time with someone like that. No plans. No ideas. Just enjoying getting to know somebody. It's been awhile.

That is really cool. You're the first newspaper designer I've ever met.

Christ, the use of the word cool again. Maybe I'm just being overly neurotic. It's probably fine. Yeah, it's fine.

Well there aren't too many of us left? What do you do?

Her on the bed. The curtains open. Me taking her from behind. Christ. I need to get my head out of the gutter.

I work for a non profit that promotes exports for U.S. wheat farmers.

I brace myself for having to explain further. I always have to explain further. At least talking with text guarantees I won't have to deal with the usual mistake. I can't count how many times I've had to explain that I'm not promoting weed exports. I have to really emphasize the T at the end. Makes me sound like an asshole. All of my friends give me shit for it.

Really? That's very cool. I grew up on a farm, my dad's a farmer.

Another cool thing you don't often get in Portland, girls who grew up on farms.

Small world. Here in North Dakota?

Yep.

I'm not sure what else to say. I know what I want to ask, but I'm not sure whether or not it's a good idea. Whatever happens, I need to take that next step. Nothing happens if I don't make the next move. Is it too soon? Not sure what else I'm going to say to a complete stranger via text. As with before, the beer in my belly is my friend again. I type out a message, then erase it. It needs to be direct, but non-threatening. I type it out again, and hit send before I can give it another thought.

A bit out of left field given I'm leaving on Wednesday, but would you be interested in getting a drink or something sometime before I leave? No expectations of course. But it does grow tiring talking to the same people at every meeting I go to.

No answer. Five minutes. Nothing. Ten minutes. Nada. Fifteen minutes. Shit. I check my phone again and again. Letting it go to sleep. Waking it up. Letting it go to sleep again. Too soon. I asked too soon. I fucked it up. I brush my teeth and get ready for bed. I turn off the lights and climb beneath the covers. My phone dings.

Sure, why not!

Hot damn. Yes, she said yes, and with an exclamation mark to boot. No, don't think too far into it. Women are always using exclamation points in texts. God only knows why. Some just use them all the damn time. Still though, she said yes.

When works for you? My meetings are noon to five tomorrow.

That's not entirely true. Those are just the meetings that I most definitely cannot miss. Silence again. Part of me is excited, the other part just wants to get everything set up so I can go to bed already. It's already a little past midnight.

Are you a night owl? Because I'll be working until about 11:30-12:00 tomorrow night but I can meet up after.

Midnight tomorrow. Holy shit. I'm here for work. I'm thirty-three. Meeting up with someone at midnight to hang out for a couple of hours does not sound all that great. Fuck it though. You know what, I'm trying to branch out, get myself out of my comfort zone. If midnight is when she can do it, then damn it, I'll manage.

I can manage. What's good in this town?

A long pause again. Damn it, I just want to go to bed. If I have to stay up past midnight tomorrow, I definitely want to get my sleep tonight.

Where are you staying?

The Ramada.

Ohhhh way over by the mall, huh. Most of the good places are downtown.

Shit. That might fuck the whole thing up. How the hell am I going to get out and back? Part of me wonders why she won't offer me a ride, even though I know why. She doesn't know me. What if I turn out to be a creeper. Who wants to give a creeper a ride back to their hotel after a creepy date?

Does Uber still run that late?

Yep. I'm pretty sure it runs at least until 2:00 when the bars close.

Problem solved.

I should be all right getting downtown then. I took it downtown yesterday, though granted, that was in the early evening.

Lets see...Sidestreet is a pretty good place. Where did you go when you came downtown before?

I hesitate in giving a full answer. The bar we went to after dinner was pretty divey. I don't want to give her the wrong idea. Fuck it though. Honesty is the best policy as they say.

It was Holo, or Hono or something like that. Then a cheaper bar down the street.

I scroll through Google Maps and look for bars in Fargo.

Hodo. Then Empire Tavern.

A long pause again. My mind drifts again to things of a sexual nature. I quickly clamp it down.

Wow, you really went from one end of the spectrum to the other that night! Lol.

Another exclamation point. Why does the sentence get one and not the LOL? It's like a monotone laugh. I'm overthinking it again.

Ha. Yep yep.

Well, Sidestreet is a pretty good middle ground, and it shouldn't be crazy busy/loud on a Tuesday.

I look at Google Maps again. There it is. Pretty easy to find.

Sounds like a plan then. See you tomorrow at midnight.

Sounds good!

Have a good night!

I go to sleep feeling a greater sense of accomplishment than anything in my business career. That stuff is easy. This is exhausting.

The meetings the next day break early, so I change into my workout clothes and go for a run. It's hot, probably close to ninety. The sweat pours from my face, but I trudge my way forward, following 42nd Street south over the freeway. The world around Fargo is flat, and the city has poured itself out into a thin layer covering a large area. The West Acres Mall, surrounded by its sea of asphalt, quickly gives way to housing developments and cookie cutter apartment buildings. The blocks are large, isolated buildings surrounded by wide swaths of grass. The street I run alongside is a major thoroughfare, four lanes wide, and the occupants of every car turn their heads as they go past. The sidewalk is largely deserted. Most people are hiding in air conditioned boxes. I meet with few others on my trek, a few other half crazy runners, and one old man on a bike. The rest are waiting for the sun to kiss the horizontal horizon, waiting for the brief period of perfect temperature before nightfall.

After less than a mile I'm sweating heavily. I drop into a walk and wipe my face with the bottom of my shirt. I walk for a while, run a bit, and then walk again. I set goals. Run to this point and you can walk to the next intersection. A blonde, a little thick but in an attractive sort of way, runs by going the opposite direction. I look her up and down behind sweat stained sunglasses. She looks at me out of the corner of her hazel eye, wary as a cat. I exceed my running goal for that portion. I'm careful not to overdo it. I don't want to wear myself out. I want to save some energy for the sex I'm not going to try to have. I can see her as I run. In the pictures she had a nice set of legs. Beautiful thighs and calves. I can't stand a skinny leg. I run and walk in a straight line for three and a half miles, then turn back to run and walk the other way.

The back of my shirt is soaked in sweat. As I approach the hotel I notice the hole in my shirt. The hole's been there for quite awhile. It's never bothered me before, but here I'm supposed to be something different. I'm supposed to be a professional. It's stupid. Why should I be someone that I'm not? A gust of wind blows by and I feel a cool cloying on the back of my shorts. They're soaked with ass sweat. The hole in my shirt doesn't seem so important.

With every step closer to the hotel the images from the dating app fill a greater portion of my mind. Tonight. It's going to be tonight. Midnight. Fuck that's late. I'm going to be tired. I should take a nap. I should probably go have dinner with some of the other people at the conference. The dinners are important, probably more important than the meetings, but not really to me. I'll take a nap. It will be better if I take a nap. I won't be so zonked out tomorrow. Maybe I should get some condoms. I'm not planning on anything happening. Hell, it couldn't be further from my mind. I'm not one of those kind of guys. But what if something did happen? Let's be honest, I sure as hell wouldn't say no. What then? I'd feel pretty stupid not having some condoms. It would be easier if women just carried condoms. It would probably make more sense. After all, they're the one taking the biggest risk. What if I was just some asshole. You know, the type who would just up and run off at the first sign of trouble. I'm not of course, but you know, what if I was? God, never suggest that to a woman, them carrying condoms that is. I've never seen some people get so worked up. Just like the damn toilet seat. I have no plans on anything happening, so why give it another thought?

I go past the hotel. It's an extra mile round trip to get to the Walgreens. It's only three blocks away. The guy behind the counter gives me a weird look as I walk in. I search through the aisles until I find what I'm looking for. I have a sweaty ten dollar bill in my pocket. I grab a small box of three of the brand I prefer and go back to the counter. I always feel weird about buying condoms. I'm thirty-three fucking years old, it really doesn't seem to be hangup I oughta have. The guy behind the counter runs my purchase and somehow seems to roll his eyes without actually doing so. I hand him my sweaty ten dollar bill. He doesn't try to hide his distaste. He doesn't even wait for me to leave to go for the hand sanitizer. His discomfort makes me feel better. It puts us on a more even playing field.

I walk back with my purchase safely hidden away in a paper bag. Past Target, Arby's, and the biggest and nicest looking cash for gold place I've ever seen. Cars streak past. I can feel the ass sweat on the back of my shorts. There's nothing I can do, so I just ignore it. I keep my eyes out for anyone I might know in the patios of the Buffalo Wild Wings and Shotgun Sallys. Nobody. The lobby of the hotel is mostly empty, only one clump of people I know off to the side. I ride the elevator alone and make it to the safety of my room.

When I get out of the shower I find a text on my phone. It's from the poor strung along girl back home. She's a nice girl. Sometimes too nice. Nice to the point where you know you're never going to be as nice as her, so every nice thing she does makes you feel guilty.

Hope the meetings are going well.

Fuck. I better answer. Sometimes we sleep together, it goes in waves. I usually try to stop because it makes me feel bad, but the intimacy is nice. Someone always checking up on me. Someone showing an interest in all my stupid shit. I try to never let it go too far, though that's exactly what has happened. She's made it no secret that she has deeper feelings for me than I'm willing to return. It would probably just be easier to give in. It wouldn't be a bad life. She'd make a pretty good wife. I don't know. Just another mess back home.

Meetings have been going well. Just got back from a run. How has work been on your end?

Been good. Jim is an asshole, but otherwise going well. Glad your day is going well. Soon enough you'll be home.

There's a smiley face at the end of her message. I answer with one of my own. It's easier that way. She's a nice girl. She deserves to be treated nicely. Hell, it's better than anything I ever got. My thoughts drift back to the girl I'm going to be seeing tonight. Maybe I should feel guilty, but I don't. I do feel guilty about not feeling guilty. It's weird. I don't know. I set the alarm on my phone and get under the covers to take a nap. A couple memories from five years ago bubble up, but I knock them back down with thoughts of the girl from the dating app. It does no good. The memories rise again. Her eying a frilly dress that looked like it was straight out of the twenties. She would've looked good in it. Her shaking in my arms, or was I shaking in her arms? Sometimes it had been hard to tell. I loved her god damn it. I didn't know you could love somebody like that. No use in thinking about it. Just have to keep moving forward.

I wake up around eight, have some food delivered to my room, and sit around and watch some TV. My eyes keep going back to the red light of the digital clock. At eleven I shower again, shave, and put on a nice pair of jeans and a t-shirt. I have to wear nice button down shirts all day. I'll be damned if I do it on my time. I don't bother combing my hair. I keep it short. There's a hell of a lot less of it than there used to be. On the plus side, losing your hair certainly helps hide the gray. With everything ready I hurry up and wait. I refuse to look at the digital clock. I check my phone instead. Around 11:30 a message pops up on Bumble.

Hey, I'm going to be stuck at work for awhile, we're having some problems with the press. I don't think I'm going to to make it out to meet you for a drink tonight, I'm sorry! If you end up back in ND again, you should definitely send me a message.

There's a winky face at the end. Fuck.

Sorry to hear, but no worries. Shit happens.

Hell, she probably got cold feet. Maybe. Maybe not. Who knows. Nothing much I can do. Tomorrow afternoon I head out for my drive around Lake Superior. Tomorrow, four and a half hours to Duluth; Thursday, eleven hours to Sault Ste. Marie; Friday, seven and a half hours back to Duluth; Saturday morning drive back to Fargo; and Saturday afternoon fly back home. All that buildup, and for what, nothing, that's what. Well shit, what can anyone do? Nothing, that's what. No, that's not right. Hell, I'm already driving all day Thursday, why not just do the same thing Friday? Why not just come straight through to Fargo? Hell, what's the harm in asking her? If she's gotten cold feet, she's gotten cold feet. Asking her isn't going to change anything. I'm not going to be in Fargo again in probably over a year. I'm not losing anything by asking.

I'm driving through Minnesota and Wisconsin over the next couple of days, then flying out of Fargo on Saturday. Would Friday evening work? If not, I'll definitely send you a message next time I make it out here. If you ever make it to Portland let me know.

212

I don't know why I lie about where all I'm going. There's really no need for it. I like to take long drives by myself for god awful long amounts of my time. What's so wrong with that? You know, aside from the fact that it sounds like something a serial killer would do. My message sits unanswered for close to fifteen minutes. Part of me can see her scurrying around, desperately trying to fix the press so they can get the paper out by morning. Another part sees her looking at her phone with disgust at the message from the desperate jackass on the other end.

Yeah, Friday could work. I don't work Fridays.

Hot damn. It worked. It really worked.

No Saturday edition, huh? I should be back in town around 7. I'll look forward to it.

Oh there's a Saturday edition. I'm just not responsible for it. ;) Have a good drive!

Thanks. Good luck with the press.

I go to bed feeling happy. Nothing risked, nothing gained. This isn't like me. When was the last time I took a risk like this? It's been awhile. Five years awhile.

The last half day of meetings go quickly. I don't bother to eat lunch. I change my clothes, check out, and catch the first hotel bus to the airport. It's the same zit covered driver. He wipes his nose with the back of his hand and we head out on our way. The grass around the airport is just as green as the day I landed.

The rental car desk is busy, though by busy I mean the people who work there are rather slow. They're in a position of power, so they get to go at the speed they prefer. Getting up to the front of the line and checking in takes forty-five minutes or so. During the check-in they demand two phone numbers. I politely inform them that I only have one phone number, but they insist that they can't rent me a car unless I have two. I tell them exactly what my opinion is of that dumb ass policy. It does little to change the problem, so I make up one off the top of my head. They're glad to be rid of me, you can see the disappointment in their eyes when I come back in. The car they gave me doesn't have a license plate. They send someone out to check it with me, you know, in case I'm a pathological liar, and then tape a temporary up in the back window. It doesn't seem very legit, but I'm tired of arguing, so I get in and head out on my way.

It's a small car. A little two door Yaris, a go-kart on steroids. There's not much to say about the drive. Fun fact, there's no direct way to drive across Minnesota from Fargo to Duluth. You have to zig zag your way across the state. It's a lot of different highway numbers to keep track of. Four and a half hours of driving. The country around Fargo is nothing but flat fields of corn and wheat, mountainous clouds stretching across the horizon up into the heavens. The monotony is broken by the occasional town, prominently marked by tall grain elevators of steel and concrete, towering above tractor dealerships, schools emblazoned with fighting mascots of one type or another, gas stations, and cafes not redecorated since the seventies. Between the towns are scattered farmsteads. Dilapidated two story houses in need of a new coat of paint, covered in an assortment of antenna and satellite dishes, surrounded by rusted metal buildings and dusty barns built by grandfathers. The grand halls of the hardy men and women who whip the land into shape. Lords with dirty faces who look up and watch as you drive past, assessing whether you are known and deserve a wave, or a stranger who gets ignored.

The farther west you go the more the trees condense. They sneak up on you. At first they are only in the towns and at the farms. Then they fill the land between the fields. Before you know it things have switched, and the fields are carved out clearings in the trees. At first it is mostly just the sleepers. Oak, poplar, walnut, maple, and cottonwood. They give way to the ones that never sleep. Pine, spruce, cedar, and hemlock. Then the fields are gone, and the dark masses on either side are broken only by the occasional lake or marsh. Some it's hard to tell the difference. There are trees as far as the eye can see, which isn't far, because of all the fucking trees.

Highway 10 to Detroit Lakes. Highway 34 to Walker. Don't go all the way to Walker. Take the cutoff to Highway 200. She'll take you all the way in until you find Highway 2. Traffic is a little slow after the cutoff. Big folk festival at the Indian casino. Campers and cars filling the road, all waiting to be let into an empty flat filled with tents and a large stage on one end. Plastic pennants flutter on the perimeter. I keep going. The traffic thins back out.

A little over three hours in I cross the mighty Mississippi, king of all the rivers, or would it be queen? Rivers seem pretty hermaphroditic. Last February I was in New Orleans. The Mississippi there has to be close to a mile wide. Here I could probably jump it if I got a good run at it. I think about stopping to do just that, or at least to take a picture, but I don't, I'm not really in the mood. I'm in the driving groove. No thoughts. No worries. No concerns. Just miles of highway falling away behind me. My phone plays podcasts jacked directly into the car's speakers. A nice feature. You can't do it with my car at home. There I just have to put my phone in a bowl so I can hear it above the bumps and rattles. When the phone loses signal, as it does from time to time, I sit in silence, startled by the sudden return when it finally reconnects. It's nice from time to time to feel numb.

Duluth is a pile of bricks on a hillside, slowly falling into the westernmost point of the Great Lakes. The cityscape is dotted with abandoned smokestacks, angry fingers defiantly flipping off the sky, outdone by the regiment of radio and cell phone towers that project themselves from the crests of the hilltops above the city. It seems like a tired city. A middle aged man who's worked long on the docks, trapped in a mid-life crisis, desperate to reinvent itself, make itself more than just its job, but unsure how, trying desperately to ignore the fact that without the docks it has no reason for existing. A row of grain terminals line the harbor. Sentinels still standing proud amongst the ruins.

My hotel, which despite the used nomenclature is actually a motel, is less than to be desired. Though to be fair, it is only seventy dollars a night. The description of Google claimed it had great access to downtown and modern rooms. It most certainly is in downtown, but modern is more in the sense that it has running water and a TV with a remote. The floors are concrete covered in outdoor carpet. The walls are stained. Everything looks washed, but not cleaned. It feels like staying at the house of an elderly aunt. A life still carrying on, though with little input since the Carter administration. For Duluth, it feels just right.

Not anxious to hang out in my room, I venture out into the maze of brick edifices that make up the downtown. It is cold outside. Bundled people hustle out from the closing businesses. Everything feels like it could use a good sweeping. On one building I note a sign with a radioactive symbol pointing out the location of a fallout shelter. Thank goodness if the worst ever happened the people of Duluth would still survive. I work my way down the hill and cross the freeway into the revitalized part of town, a small spit and polished nub jutting out into the lake. Nice hotels, chain restaurants, and brewpubs. People sitting outside, laughing and chatting, their eyes locked out at the lake, never looking back, discussing the reincarnation of their town.

On the very end of the nub is the entrance to the harbor, the gap crossed by a lifting bridge, the other side a long spit covered by big expensive looking houses. Despite the riches on the other side, the bridge is raised, waiting for a huge freighter to come in, even the wealthy powerless against the demands of commerce. People line the jetty, cameras out, taking pictures as the behemoth slowly makes its way in. Smaller boats pull alongside and zip away. I watch with all the rest, taking my own photos. Lake Superior stretches out before me like the ocean, but with no waves beating against its shores. It is only brought to life by storms. The ship makes its way into the harbor, the bridge drops back into place, and the crowd disperses to continue on with their day. I wander into a nearby maritime museum and let a lonely curator discuss the finer points of steam engines with me before getting bored and starting my way back up the hill.

The sun disappears behind the antennas. The downtown is empty and dark, just a few tweakers moving aimlessly. One follows me for a couple of blocks, but then gets bored, or distracted, and heads off in a different way. I stop at what claims to be a Thai restaurant not far from my hotel and order some food to go. The painting of a Thai village on their wall is exactly like the one in the Thai restaurant near my house in Portland. I take my food and go back to my motel room. The food is nothing like the place in Portland. A poor facsimile based more on pictures than actual taste, and the pictures must have not been that good either. I eat all of it, flipping through channels. I wish someone was here with me. With somebody else I could go out and have an adventure. With just me, I just watch TV.

After I eat I use my computer to change my hotel reservation for Friday night from Duluth to Fargo. I find a nice hotel in downtown, walking distance to the Sidestreet. I look at Amy's pictures on Blurb. She has a nice smile. It's a warm smile. Not a forced one. Not a mask put on for the camera. Genuine. She has a nice figure. Thin and lithe. Beautiful. Pressed up against me. Her long fingers play their way across me. Our lips touch, pull back, and touch again. I rub her back. She likes it. I offer to give her a massage. She strips out of her clothes. She lets her bra fall to the ground. I'm on top of her, kneading her back, she lets out an involuntary moan. Things escalate quickly.

This is no fantasy. I've been here before. Only the actors have changed. A nice girl back home. An understudy, filling in until the star arrives, waiting for her big chance that will never come. I stop myself, but then keep going. What's it matter? What's it matter if I masturbate to a woman that I don't know beyond a few pictures and a few messages back and forth? What does it hurt? Nothing, that's what. Nothing at all. I'm no fool. I know the difference between what is real and what is imaginary. I know that the simplicity of the mind will never be the world around me. Damn it. Must I feel guilty for everything? Must I deny this basic carnal biology? Can I not even be a beast when alone in this dingy motel room? Her legs tighten around me. Fuck it. Her fingernails claw my back. Take it. Heavy breathing in my ear. Do it. Spasm. Nothing. I'm alone again. Just me and a wad of toilet paper filled with goo sitting on a comforter that smells faintly of cigarettes.

The alarm on my phone wakes me up at six. It's still pretty dark out. I go in the bathroom and flip the switch. Nothing. I go into the main living room and try the lamp. Nothing. The power is out. The bathroom is nearly pitch black. I pee by the light of my phone, consider my options with showering, and decide it's not the end of the world to skip it. Unless I get a wild hair up my ass and pick up a hitchhiker, it doesn't really matter. I pack my bags, put them in the car, and go into the office to return my key. A fat man sits behind the desk, munching on a danish. An old man sits and stares at the blank TV hung from a corner. The fat man brushes crumbs off of his chin onto my receipt.

"No breakfast, powers out."

I raise my eyebrows a bit and nod my understanding.

"Yep."

I take a banana muffin from the counter next to the coffee machine as I leave. I only eat half of it. The other half gets thrown out onto the highway only a couple miles outside of

Duluth. Interstate 35 gives out, turning into Highway 61, which winds its way through residential areas spilled along the lake. There must have been a storm last night. The highway is littered with a thick carpet of green leaves. Tree branches litter the sidewalks and streets. Early morning crews are already busy with buzzing saws, clearing the biggest chunks out of the way. I didn't hear a thing. I must have slept like a baby, minus the waking up in the middle of the night screaming and shitting myself.

Intermixed pines and birches whip by to either side, breaking from time to time to give a view of the lake, its waters dancing with the light of the rising sun. The highway condenses down from four lanes to two. There is nothing here, just empty road. the occasional green sign or row of mailboxes giving clues to the existence of habitation hidden out of sight against the lake. I stop for a bit at a state park named after a lighthouse, which is in turn named after a split rock, to get out and stretch my legs. The lake looks serene. If she threw a fit the other day, it's hard to tell. It's close to three hours to the Canadian border. Two Harbors. Illgen. Taconite Harbor. Grand Marais. Sleepy little towns waking up to greet the day. My personal favorite is Castle Danger. It sounds like something out of a Monty Python sketch. The type that would use a high pitched voice with a bad British accent, strained hoarse by a screaming whisper.

"Castle Danger it is me lord, nobody goes there. Nobody."

I enjoy it for a couple of miles.

The Canadian border agent has thick mascara around beautiful green eyes that look half dead. She's in full work mode. Running on automatic. Even with the bulk of the bulletproof vest she's attractive. I hand over my passport and she types on her keypad, keeping half her attention on me to spot any suspicious behavior.

"What are you coming into Canada for?"

"I'm driving around Lake Superior."

219

"How long do you plan on being in Canada?"

"A couple of days."

"Why doesn't your car have license plates?"

"It's the one the rental car company gave me. They put a temporary in the back window."

I hand her my pink copy of the rental agreement. She takes it and looks it up and down.

"Do you have any weapons, drugs, alcohol, fruits, or vegetables?"

"No."

She hands me back the pink and my passport.

"Welcome to Canada."

"Thank you."

She doesn't answer. I put the car back into gear and move forward. A sign politely reminds me that the speed is 90 kilometers per hour, otherwise the road looks basically the same. It's an hour drive from the border to Thunder Bay, the last major city before the push around the northern half of the lake on Highway 17. Seven and a half hours, without stops, between Thunder Bay and Sault Ste. Marie on the lake's eastern end.

Thunder Bay is Duluth's cousin, same look, but not contained by the encircling hills, instead spilled across the flats. Canadian entry point to the Great Lakes. Little in it is worth remembering. As I make my way from stoplight to stoplight I spot the Google Maps car with its three hundred and sixty degree camera mast. I raise my middle finger in salute until it falls behind. A car pulls ahead of me, a modified Cadillac with the front seat roof cutoff to form a convertible, a spoiler bolted onto the back. I laugh and struggle to both drive and take a picture with my phone. It doesn't come out well. A few more stoplights and I leave Thunder Bay behind.

The lake peeps out from time to time, but mostly it's just trees, miles and miles of trees. Sometimes there's traffic, sometimes not. It seems to go in waves. The road goes straight, but my mind wanders. Tomorrow evening I'll be back in Fargo, and if things go right, out getting drinks with a pretty blonde haired girl I've never met. Maybe we'll hit it off. Maybe she'll take me home, or I'll take her back to my hotel room. Maybe it will be more than just genitals slapping together. Maybe it will be what I'm looking for.

We part ways in the morning. I have to go home, back to Portland. I don't want to go, and I can tell that she feels the same, but life is what it is. I can't stop thinking about her the whole flight home. I'm not sure what to do. Part of me tells me it's nothing. Another declares it's everything. A risk. I have to take a risk. After two days I give her a call. How'd I get her phone number? We traded numbers when I left. She wanted me to call. I just had to get up the balls to do it. It's a funny story about how two people met. A good one. It's awkward at first. I've never been one for talking on the phone. We talk for hours. We talk every day. I send her texts wishing her a good morning. She sends me texts asking about my day. It's awkward. We either have to talk in the later afternoon or late at night to work around her job. Phone calls give way to Skype. It's good to see her face again, her figure, her smile. Sometimes we do more than just talk. We're adults. It's how it works, but it's not just that. I can see it in her eyes. I wonder if she can see it in my eyes too. We both talk about how much we wish we could see each other again. After three months she comes to visit. I show her around. We revel in each other's presence. We fuck like animals. It comes time for her to go. I don't want her to go. I don't think she wants to go either. It's time for another risk. I force the words out of my mouth. She doesn't have to go. This can be her home. She agrees. She's excited, but also scared, just like me.

I'm not insane. I know that I don't even know this person, that I'm constructing a fantasy on a foundation of nothing, but it's nice, it's a nice fantasy. Is it wrong? Is it wrong to construct such a world when you don't even believe in it yourself? The girl back home would be hurt. She's a nice girl. All she wants is the same thing that I do. I just don't think I'm the one that can give it to her. Sometimes she's too nice. What the hell does she want with me? I have no plans on marrying her. Hell, I've made that apparent more times than I can count, but still she's there. Waiting. Hoping. What does she want with someone like me? Doesn't she know any better? What the hell am I doing with her? I know the answer to that. I know the bars of the cage that I've built for myself. I know that this evening she'll have sent me another text, telling me that she hopes I had a great day. I know that I'll answer. I'm not so far gone that I'm able to hurt on a whim. I know how it feels to be on the other end.

I stop in some little nowhere town for lunch. A drive-in where the road forks. It's pretty much just a trailer with picnic tables out front. The owner runs the grill while high school girls take and deliver orders, waiting in hopes that their zit covered dreamboats will stop by. I get a mushroom swiss burger, sit at a table, and read a book. An old couple stop to eat. They ask far too many questions about the food and get in a quiet debate over whether to get one order of fries or two. The woman insists she won't eat enough to make ordering two necessary. The man insists she will. It's not a real fight. More like a loving discussion. A family arrives in a minivan, three kids, two boys and a girl. The boys are rambunctious, running around like half wild animals, only the threat of no ice cream from their father's throat slowing them down. The daughter is precocious, staring out at the world with wide brown eyes. The parents look dull eyed and tired, but strangely content with the creations they have wrought.

The last to arrive is a young couple. He gets out first. It's obvious that he works out, but pretty much only his arms. His bulging biceps and triceps are covered in tribal tattoos. His ears are full of earrings. His head is shaved. His eyes are hidden by

mirrored sunglasses. He wears combat boots with shorts. He
looks like a douchebag. She gets out as he stalks off to the find
the bathroom. She's young, probably early twenties, and has the
body to prove it. She wears a tight tank top that leaves nothing
to the imagination. Flat stomach below two perfect orbs that
have no business being on a girl of her size. No bra holds them
back. They press against the slim fabric of her top. Sweatpants
cover a nice round ass. Her hair is pulled back into two tight
braided pigtails. I feel bad for the douchebag. This girl is
nothing but trouble. The kind that will blow your mind, but fuck
with your head. She knows what she has, and she looks at the
world as nothing but a tray of morsels from which she gets to
select the choicest pieces. Don't like it? Too bad for you. Her
cup will never run dry. Empathy is for those that nature scorned.

Nobody has the power not to stare. The old man chews fries
next to his oblivious wife. The married man sucks on his soda,
unaware of his wife's dirty looks. I go with the long glance,
look away, and glance again method. The douchebag comes
stalking back. He catches me looking. I can feel his eyes on me.
Sizing me up. I look away. He looks like the kind who likes to
start a fight. I've never been much of a fighter. I throw my trash
away and get back on the road. Poor bastard. That sorry son of
a bitch.

She comes a few weeks later. She quits her job, loads all of
her stuff in a U-Haul, and makes the journey west. I clear out a
place for her in my life. I throw out the things in my house that
are there not because I really need them, but just because I have
the space for them to sit. It's a whole new world. My friends
and family don't understand. They think I'm acting crazy. I
don't know a damn thing about this girl, but I answer that I know
enough. It's a hard adjustment. It's hard for her to find work,
she has to do a couple less than perfect fit jobs, retail and the
such, before landing one she likes. It soon becomes obvious that
both of us have lived alone for quite some time. Habits

developed over the years are hidden, revealed, and adjusted. Sometimes we fight. One time the fight gets so bad that she yells that moving was a mistake and I stalk out into the night so I don't punch a hole in the wall. When I come back she's crying. I say I love you for the first time. The first time in a long time those words have passed my lips. She loves me too. We fight to make it work. There's plenty of good times, more than I can count, but it is our reaction to the bad times that defines us, that melds us into a unit. We never stop fighting. We've both found something worth fighting for. We marry in less than a year. The first baby comes along in less than two. We have to adjust again. I'm not happy, but I'm content, and in the end, it's what really matters.

By early afternoon Highway 17 works its way away from the lake into the empty nothing of coniferous trees and lakes that are more marsh than pond until turning south for the final run through provincial parks to Sault Ste. Marie. I need to get gas. The small towns dribble out without a gas station in sight. There's one on the side of the road at the edge of the last. I miss it. Oh well, I probably have enough to make it to where the highway turns south. The map claims there's a town. Maybe I made the wrong choice. Maybe there's nothing there. It's been that way a couple of times. Dots on the map that turn out to be just a collection of sad houses and dilapidated boarded up businesses. Even in their heyday they weren't much. I don't have enough if there's nothing there. I don't want to go back. Going forward is always better than going back. Never go backwards. You should never go back. Good sense wins the day. I turn around and return to the gas station. Inside the convenience store they have Crystal Clear Pepsi. They haven't made it since the mid-nineties. What the hell is it doing here? I buy it and a bag of chips. It does not taste good. Back to the road. Back to moving on.

How was it that the nice girl back home became part of my life? How long has it been? Years now. It doesn't seem that long. It started as a one night stand that just kept going. At first it was only sex, just like all the others, but I could see the growth inside of her. The need for something more. I knew I had to run, but something held me back. A need that I had forsaken. A want that I had all but forgotten. Intimacy. Knowing someone else and having them know you. Feeling something besides lust. She was an innocent, something inside of her had survived the world so far. How could I be the one to hurt her? I did. I hurt her many times, but always I came back, and always she welcomed me in once again, her arms held out open wide. I changed, whether I wanted to or not. I changed so that I wouldn't hurt her. I'd hurt enough, excuses of my own pain upon my lips. I changed until I could not change anymore, and though it was not enough to grant her wish, she stayed, both of us stuck in limbo until the end of time.

Our second child comes two years after the first. It's getting crowded in our little house. She wants to move, maybe to the suburbs. I don't. I want to stay exactly where we are. Damn the neighborhood. Damn the schools. This is mine, and nobody will ever take it from me. We argue, we divide, but in the end we come together. I quit my job and find another. I tell my boss exactly what I think of him. It feels good. She supports me. We don't leave the house, at least not until another year later, when the world has settled and we find ourselves able to consider it once again. We move, not to the suburbs, but to a better area, into a better house, one with a big yard. It's on the edge of our price range. We get caught up in our own worlds. We drift apart, but find each other again, pull ourselves back together. We make love with a passion as though it's the first time. I love her. God damn it how I love her.

The highway bends to the south and I follow, a retreat from the wilds of the woods, back to the definitive line of the lakeshore. I re-listen to podcasts that flowed in one ear and out the other. I laugh at myself. I laugh at the ridiculousness of it all. A fantasy of a girl who doesn't exist except in a few pictures and a couple of texts. It all has to start somewhere though. It all has to have a beginning. Nothing is going to start unless I try. Signs flash by alongside the road. White splotches of a dragon beneath Agawa Rock in big white letters. The miles beneath tick down, thirty, twenty, ten, and then there it is. An arrow pointing me off my path. An arrow leading down towards the lake. I take it. I need to get out of this car. I've been sitting in it far too long. I'm restless, every bone in my body quivering with unreleased energy.

It's a secluded gravel parking lot, surrounded by trees, only two other cars. Next to one is a young couple, changing out of hiking shoes into flip flops. I park my rental and get out. The young couple eye me warily. It's quiet here. We're at least half a mile off the highway. Even the birds seem subdued. I walk over to read the tall sign next to a gravel path leading off into the trees. Agawa Rock, site of cliff paintings done by the Ojibwe. A sacred spot for at least 1,500 years along Gitchee Gummee, the Ojibwe name for Lake Superior, better than the boring anglicized name chosen because it was bigger than all the rest. The young couple get into their car and drive away. The birds start singing again. I set out down the path. The sign said it would be a little under a mile.

The coniferous trees are tall and block out the sun. The trail winds its way through their shadows, turning to mud in places, others blocks of solid stone. It's under this thick blanket that I meet a woman around my age coming the other way. The appearance of another startles us both, and we stop with ten feet between us. I give a friendly nod and an attempt at a half smile. She looks nervous. Her eyes dart from me to the surrounding trees and back again. I know what the problem is. I'm a lone man and she's a lone woman. It is the way of the world.

Sometimes the path is too narrow, and allowances have to be made. I step aside, try to smile again, and gesture for her to pass. She comes forward, as unsure as a deer. I'm not sure what to do. Should I watch her pass, or should I look away? Should I try to say something? Should I slouch and try to make myself look small? All of this thinking about it probably does little to help. People can tell when you're over thinking things. Over thinking things is always dangerous. She passes by and moves up the trail. I head my own direction. I don't look back.

The path scrambles over some rocks and down a staircase cleverly built in a cut. At the bottom is the cliffs. They're tall. Probably close to a hundred feet high. A huge slab of granite proudly jutting itself into the blue waters of Gitchee Gummee. Small islands of rock and pines sit out in the water. The rocks are covered by neatly stacked stone cairns. Why do fucking tourists always feel the need to build stone cairns wherever they go? Near the waterline the vertical drop of the cliffs softens into a shelf, a moderate six foot wide slope which drops off again down into the cold waters of the lake. A tourist display marks the end of the trail. A diagram showing the red ochre paint that can be seen on the cliff. Men in canoes, deer, horses, snakes, men with spears, fish, lizards, and grandest of them all, the dragon. It's a simple drawing. Long neck supporting a head framed by horns like a bull. Spines running down its back and tail. Next to the diagram is a stern warning to be careful on the rocks, and to most definitely not go out on them if there is a storm. The weather is clear. I should be all right.

A small set of stairs goes from the display to the shelf beneath the cliff. At the bottom of the stairs is a post with an old life preserver and rope. Large eye bolts have been driven into the granite of the shelf every eight feet or so. Chains and ropes dangle down the shelf and off the drop off into the water. Waves lap gently against the stone, the occasional wave strong enough to jangle the chains. I didn't come all this way not to see the dragon. The sloping granite is slick beneath the rubber soles of my shoes. It's hard to keep a grip in places. My hands seek out purchase along the cliffside, which juts forward overhead, an ominous beast watching me from its heights. I use the eye bolts to plant my feet. My eyes sweep across the stone, hunting amongst the orange lichen for signs of ochre red. There's a fish. There's a deer. Where is the dragon?

The eye bolts run out. I don't see it. My eyes scan the stone above me, but there's nothing there. There's more cliff ahead, but no way forward. The slope is steeper. The granite is too wet. What the fuck? Where is the dragon? I look back the way I've come. There's paintings all along the cliff. Horses, birds, men, canoes, but no dragon. It must be further ahead, but why the hell would they make it so difficult? My eyes go to my hands to re-adjust them on the cliff. Maybe if I can get better purchase I can go forward more. I don't need to. The dragon is right in front of me. My hands are just in front of it. It's sitting right at eye level. How the hell did I miss it? The damn thing is over two feet tall. The shadows. It must have been how the light was hitting the rock. I take a picture, and start monkey crawling my way back.

At the third eye bolt from the stairs my foot slips and I go down. For a moment I hang there, my hands scrabbling against unyielding stone, then my feet are moving out from under me in a slow motion plunge towards the blue water below. It doesn't hurt, but it gets my heart racing. The downward plunge is stopped by a jut of rock which halts my progress at the drop. A particularly strong wave clashes against the stone, splashing upward and wetting the cuff of my pants before it withdraws with just as quick of a motion. Gitchee Gummee looks much more powerful from this perspective. If I had fallen in she could have battered me against the cliff as she pleased. Stupid. It was stupid to come out here alone. What if something had happened? Where would I be then? The eyebolt provides me with enough leverage to get myself back onto the straight and narrow. As I re-climb the stairs a couple with two kids make their way down the trail, the father leading the way. He smiles as we pass.

"How was it?"

"Pretty cool, but pretty slick too."

The father nods in understanding. I push my way past his brood, and head back up the path to my car. I hope he doesn't try to take his kids out onto the rocks. It's his business though. It's better when one is not alone.

The pavement makes its way beneath my tires once more. No stopping now. No pausing. It's the last push to Sault Ste. Marie. One and half more hours south, racing a sun making its way towards the western horizon, burnishing the surface of the lake to a high sheen too bright to stare at for long. The car moves in silence. No radio. No podcasts. Just me watching the lines of the highway blur past. The woman from five years ago sits next to me. Her tall statuesque form folded neatly in the passenger seat. Her eyes, the color of the ocean, staring out the window as the lake moves past. I stay quiet. I want to say something, there have always been so many things that I've wanted to say, but I don't. I want her to go, but I'm scared that she will go away. She doesn't need to speak. I can hear the words in my head. Anxiety. When I'm with you I'm fine, but when you're gone I feel overwhelmed. You don't understand, don't pretend like you understand. Once I lose it, it is gone. I don't know why this happens. Quit trying to fix it.

Tears in her eyes. Tears in her eyes as she says again that she wants to break up. I give in. Tired. I'm just so very tired. I want to ask again. I want to ask the question that she'd never answer, though I knew what the answer was. Why did you break up with me? Fight. Deflect. Just say it god damn it. Say the word so oft repeated. Anxiety. No reason. There was no god damn reason. Anything. I would have done anything for you, but you threw it away. You threw it away and blamed me for things over which I had no control. She sits staring out the window and even from the corner of my eye I can see her trembling. She was always trembling, like a nervous little dog, her words, not mine. I shake in my seat. A tremor that works its way from my toes and upwards to the top of my head and out the tips of my fingers. It is just as it was before. I only dream that I could forget.

I've always been this way. I know you want to know more, but talking about it makes it worse. Avoidance, the worst thing you can do. Avoidance is the breeding ground of monsters. Avoidance allows them to grow. I don't want to remember. I don't want to forget. Contentment. That was the word whispered lying in darkness. What do you feel? Contentment. She sits and stares out the window. I want to grab her. I want to shake her. I want to yell in her face, but I don't want her to go. I don't want to see the sadness in her eyes. I want her to be happy. It's crazy to think of such things. It's been five years. Far too long to be hung up on something like this. Time heals everything. Just memories best left behind. I try to conjure up the fantasy of the girl from Fargo. We're on a date. She's laughing. Her hand finds its way to mine beneath the table. I give her fingers a squeeze. I know the look in her eyes. It's no use. The fantasy flutters and gives way, broken by the unyielding concrete of a world that really happened. She sits next to me, but can't even turn to look me in the eye.

I wish she'd turn. I wish she'd see my tears. I wish she'd hear my voice uttering the apologies. I wish I'd hear her voice uttering the same. What was I supposed to do? Everyone told me to walk away, but I couldn't, not knowing what I knew. What is the one thing that you want most in this world? Love. How can you know and do nothing? How can that be okay? She deserves everything she wants, even if it means destroying the one thing you hope down deep inside. You can pretend to be as noble as you want, but you know that it is there. A need pushed out of sight, only to escape with bubbling anger. It doesn't matter. You must do what you must do. You must nail your own hands on the martyr's cross, accept the consequences, and wonder forever if it was the right thing to do. I want you out of my life.

Does she know? Does she forgive? Does she understand? All attempts had failed. All lines of communication broken beyond repair. It is time to look forward, not back. It is time to press ahead into the great unknown. Most of it was probably in my head. I alone was yelling at the storm. It's stupid to think about. It is done, and that is that. The girl from five years ago sits next to me in silence, until traffic begins to get heavier, and then she is gone.

Ste. Sault Marie starts like most towns. An increase in roads to either side. Two lanes turn to four. Stoplights at intersections. Car dealerships, locksmiths, box stores, and strip malls. Suburban sprawl that gives way to urban. Brick houses and businesses giving way to industrial bulwarks along the waterfront. For Lake Superior, the edge of the world, it's great mass spilling downward into Lake Huron. Large locks give access to shipping between the two bodies of water, and over all of it spans two miles of steel and concrete, a connecting artery between two worlds split by imaginary lines.

My hotel is just off the waterfront. A modest L shaped two story structure with fake grecian pillars framing the doorway. I have to wait nearly half an hour to check in as a man debates with the desk clerk over the usage of coupons, online deals, and god only knows what else. His wife stands patiently to the side, repeating his words in support as needed. His kids sit in lobby chairs, bored out of their minds, but too disciplined to cause any trouble. When it's finally my turn the clerk looks apologetic.

"Sorry about that."

"No worries."

What else am I supposed to say? Some people are just that way.

Safely ensconced in my room on the second floor I change into my running clothes. I've been in the car too long. I need to run. I need to move. I need to burn off my energy. I open Bumble on my phone before I go. Her picture looks up at me. The girl from Fargo is smiling. Tomorrow. I'll be back in Fargo tomorrow.

I should be back at about 7 tomorrow. You want to meet a the Sidestreet at 7:30 so I can take a quick shower?

I put my door's keycard in my pocket, double knot my shoes, and head out the door. Evening is coming. It's not here yet, but it's definitely on its way. A path follows the waterfront. This part has been turned into a park. I head west towards the setting sun. The bridge stretches across the horizon. Tall stacks belch smoke into the darkening array of colors. Across the water, on the American side, sits the great red brick edifice of the old customs house. A monument to the days when the connection between the lakes was first conquered by canals and gates, a time when men walked taller than the trees, and with middle fingers held high made nature their bitch. I'm out of the wilds now. Back in civilization.

People stroll along the path, but I pay them no mind. They are nothing, just obstacles. The trail makes sharp ninety degree turns, maneuvering around square inlets that had use when the waterfront meant more than just a place to look at the water. One contains a marina, filled with sailboats run by motors. The water is dark blue, highlighted by reddish and orange hues dappling the surface. Tourist center. Restaurants. A half dismantled stage beneath a great canopy. It feels good to run. It feels good to stretch my legs. It's warm. Sweat flows freely. The slight sting of salt in my eyes. The park gives way to the edge of an expansive parking lot centered by a giant mall. The parking lot is mostly empty. The city is shutting down for the

night. Bikers, walkers, other runners, we all share the trail.
Some push baby carriages. Others walk in large groups that I
have to go around.

The trail turns and goes past weed filled lots. The people
disappear, only the occasional runner like myself. Lamps flicker
on overhead. A chain link fence between me and the water. The
path curves and crosses to an island. It's long and narrow. I run
to the other side. Here is the original canal and locks, built over
a hundred years ago. Far too small for the vessels of today,
relegated to pleasure craft while the titans of commerce make the
descent closer to the American side, its previous glory now
forgotten. One of the big bulk vessels emerges from the far off
locks. A massive chunk of steel holding ore, grain, or other
commodity, the basic building blocks of our society. Its engines
ramp up towards full power. Smoke billows from its stack. It
moves away into the twilight, bound for Huron and beyond.

I don't know what comes over me. I want to catch it. I want
to beat it. I turn and my feet beat a rapid staccato back the way I
came. Back across the island. Back across the bridge. Back
past the empty lots to where the crowds grow thick once again.
The light is fading. The crowds are thicker now. I juke from
side to side, passing fleshy obstacles both with and against my
current. The vessel continues moving forward, unaware of the
John Henry battling to reign supreme. Man versus machine.
Blood versus oil. The mall slides away to my left, then the
restaurants, the tourist center, and the park. The crowds thin
with the waning sunlight. There is my hotel, but still the steel
giant is winning. I keep going. Sweat pours from my brow. My
lungs are heaving. My legs feel ragged. My ankles ache. It
doesn't matter. I've tapped into something deeper. Something
more than muscle and bone. The path ends and I push on
through the grass, past apartment windows where people cook
dinners and watch television. I must catch it. I have to win.

The grass runs out. A chain link fence surrounds a big lot of sand and weeds. Not like this. I'm not going to lose like this. I turn and leave the water behind. Follow the fence away from the waterfront, up behind the apartment buildings where signs declare no trespassing. There's a low fence blocking my way, but I scramble over. Time. I'm wasting precious time. The path appears again along the street. I turn and follow it, headed in the right direction again. I can see the ship in the distance, still ahead of me. I run faster. My side aches, but I ignore it. The lot disappears and I'm against the waterfront once more. Rusted hulks sit tied up and forgotten. Bush planes sit outside of hangars. There is nobody here. Just me. Concrete gives way to weeds again, then nothing, nothing but sand and silt churned up by construction equipment. A helipad and the cracked remains of a parking lot. I'm catching the son of a bitch. I'm pulling alongside. Even with the back. Even with the middle. The front. I'm nearing the front. On its deck I can see crewmen moving, shadowy forms backlit by the ship's lights. I'm going to win. I'm going to beat this thing.

The path runs out. The waterfront takes a hard ninety degree turn and fades into the backyards of upper income homes. There is no place left to go. I stand, bent over, hands on knees, breathing hard, watching the ship slipping away into the darkness. I was even. I was doing it. So close. There's nothing to be done. It's completely dark now. Nothing but emptiness around me. This doesn't seem to be the kind of place where one wants to stick around. I make my way back to the hotel, mostly walking, but jogging from time to time.

I use my keycard to let myself into a side door. I climb the stairs to a vending machine on the landing. Chips. Candy. Granola bars. I have some money in my pocket. I try to feed the bills into the machine, but it refuses to take them. It's hot here at the top of the stairs. Ungodly hot. The machine refuses all of

my advances. I curse under my breath. A man opens the door
from the hall and moves past me. He glances at me.

"Thing don't work."

I look at him.

"What?"

He gestures at the vending machine.

"It's broken."

I nod my understanding. The man continues on his way,
down the stairs and out the side door. I'm hungry, but I
surrender. There's nothing to be done. Some things just have to
be accepted. It's late now. Most places will be closed. I don't
feel like getting back in the car. I go back to my room and shut
the door. I sit down on the bed. My sweat dries to crystals,
gritty to the touch. I check my phone. There's a text, but it's not
from the girl in Fargo. It's from the nice girl back home.

*Hope you're having a good trip and having lots of
adventures. Can't wait for you to get home.*

It's punctuated by a smiley face. I open Bumble. Nothing.
The girl from Fargo's smiling face looks up at me. The round
shape of her ass and breasts push against her dress. Long legs.
Delicate hands. I let myself go. I pummel myself with a ferocity
bordering on animalistic. I let the images come. She laughs.
She smiles. She does everything I want and more. She's a
person. Complexity. Free will. I want to fuck her. I want to
fuck her so bad. Is that so wrong? Is that so fucking wrong?
I'm a man. She's an attractive woman. Such urges are only
natural. A deep down instinct. I know it is not real. I know that
we have never met, but that matters little in this basic desire.
This is not a thing of logic. It's not a thing of emotion. It's
instinct. The foundation of it all.

It's fantasy. A world uncomplicated by the rest. An escape
until with a surge the world comes back, with all of its guilt and
shame. A return to knowing what I am. I sit on the edge of the
bed, waiting for the last of the hormones to drain away. I'm

hungry and I'm tired, but I can only solve one of these problems.
I clean up the remains of my pride and flush them down the
toilet. I rinse my hands. I brush my teeth. I set the alarm for
6:00 AM. It's a twelve hour drive back to Fargo tomorrow. I
lay in bed with my phone in my hands, tapping out a message.

*Trip is going well. Looking forward to getting home too.
How have you been?*

*Good. Work is hell. Checked your house yesterday.
Everything was fine.*

*Thanks. Going to bed now. Have to get up early tomorrow.
Have a good night.*

You too.

There is no response by morning. Getting to the bridge turns
out to be a bigger pain in the ass than expected. A lot of zigging
and zagging around blocks that seem entirely unnecessary. The
bridge rises and comes back down in a twin town of the same
name, just on the other side of the water. The U.S. border station
blocks passage off of the bridge. The border patrol agent looks
damn near identical to her Canadian counterpart in Grand
Portage, only older and more weathered. Where the Canadian
was attractive, this version appears to have melted into the
cesspit of age and unhappy living. Her body, once able to turn
heads, is now rotund, a once proud edifice collapsing in on itself.
The eyes are the same, bright green surrounded by a thick border
of mascara, peering out at the world with a tired look of
disinterest and suspicion. Even the questions are eerily the
same.

"What were you in Canada for?"

"I was driving around Lake Superior."

"How long were you in Canada?"

"A couple of days."

"Why doesn't your car have license plates?"

"It's the one the rental car company gave me. They put a
temporary in the back window."

I hand her my pink copy of the rental agreement. She takes it and looks it up and down.

"Do you have any weapons, drugs, alcohol, fruits, or vegetables?"

"No."

She hands me back the pink and my passport.

"Welcome to the United States."

"Thank you."

Highway 17 turns into Interstate 75 before you even get out of town. Four lanes of cracked pavement surrounded by a thick layer of green. Green grass. Green trees, all nearly the same shade, the monotony only broken by flashes of little white flowers. Interstate 75 is a frozen gray river that stretches 1,700 miles south to Miami. I take it for only ten before exiting onto Highway 28. Soon after the exit I stop at a convenience store to refill my gas tank and buy garbage for breakfast, a bag of powdered donuts and a bottle of juice. I leave my change in an old coffee can plastered with the face of a local man who was injured in a hunting accident.

Northern Michigan is nothing but pine, spruce, beech, and birch. A heavy blanket only broken by the occasional clearing or gravel road. Signs for RV parks and summer camps litter the side of the road. She still hasn't messaged back. I find myself checking far too often for me to be comfortable. I've been down that road before. It's not a place I want to be again. Anxiety. Such things are contagious. You spend too much time around anyone, things start to rub off. It's silly anyways. I know what's happened, I'm no idiot, but I still hold out hope. You never know. You just never know. I limit myself to only checking every two hours, though I know it will probably be every hour.

The highway hums beneath the rental car's tires, a steady snapping rhythm from when they hit the seams. I do my best to distract myself with radio and podcasts. Lull myself into a trance. Don't think. Don't think about anything. I make jokes

in my head. Terrible jokes. Jokes I would never say out loud
unless maybe drunk with my closest friends. Racist jokes.
Sexist jokes. Terrible fucking jokes. Some of them make me
laugh out loud. They're funny. Not in a pleasant chuckle way.
More in a you're not supposed to say, or even think, things like
that sort of way. A big middle finger to society as a whole. It's
empowering. Like yelling a slur where nobody can hear. Say it.
Handle it. See that it has no power beyond what we give it, and
throw it away.

The road is still surrounded by a single shade of green.
Railroad tracks parallel on the left side. Here and there a town
brushes by. Small ones, just a quick collection of houses and
businesses. Big ones, with box stores crowding the edges and
stoplights stuttering the flow. There's no messages on my phone
and that's all right. Tomorrow I'll fly home and all such dreams
will be done, banished back into the realm of reality. It was late
when I sent it, maybe she was too busy at work. Nothing this
morning makes sense, if I worked until midnight or later I'd
probably sleep in too. I stop at another convenience store for
lunch. Chips, jerky, and a pop. I don't have time to slow down
or stop. I have to keep moving forward. Each hour forward is
another slim shaving off of my hope. Another piece of
reasoning knocked flat. In the middle of the date she puts her
hand on mine, and it's a shock to realize there's something there.
A silly thought for a wandering mind. Pathetic. I brush it away
with all the rest.

The pine and hemlock begin to fall back, but the oak, elm,
and maple rise up to take their place. There are scattered houses
now. Newspaper and mail boxes at the end of driveways. For a
short bit I'm against the lake again, and then it's gone, bending
away from the straight line of the highway. The pine and
hemlock reclaim their dominance, but the single shade of green
is gone, replaced by an undulating pool of greens, browns, and
yellows. Low slung power lines hang from bleached out poles.

Maybe they're old telephone lines. They seem too low for power lines. The trees fall back again as the highway crosses into Wisconsin. A thin blue line runs across the northern horizon, visible across mowed fields filled with round bales and abandoned shining new tractors. Farmsteads marked by big red barns and the tall silvery tubes of granaries, capped by rounded tops.

The trees come back, mostly beech and maple, locked in a struggle of dominance with the clearings made long ago to allow the land to be tilled and cultivated. It all brushes past, flashing by for a second before being forgotten once again. The lake pulls away again, one last bend before it returns for the last time. The car works its way through the streets of Superior, before crossing into the outskirts of Duluth. There is no message. It is done. I have rounded the lake. My endeavor ends without passion, only a dull thud of completion and the knowledge that I must remember it, for I will likely never pass this way again.

I drive west across Minnesota via the same route that I went east two days before. With nothing new to look at, my brain is finally allowed to collapse into a stupor, where only the parts necessary for driving maintain any kind of activity. I stop at the Mississippi River to stretch my legs. A voice in my head tells me to jump in, the voice that has no awareness of consequence or danger. I ignore it. The brown water looks cold. There's a chill wind in the air. At the Indian reservation halfway across it looks like the folk festival is getting into full swing. Thousands of sparks flitting wildly with one another, desperate to taste life before they burn out. Maybe there's a spark in there for me. Two sparks can create a fire, an inferno, but how would you know? A million paths to take, but only one to follow. I keep going.

I refuse to look at my phone. The highway winds its way down onto the cultivated flats before Fargo. It's been raining here. There is water in the ditches and puddles on the road. The asphalt gleams as though freshly scrubbed, steam rising from its surface. Clouds as big as mountains roll past. The podcast is about a shut-in. He goes out, but never lets anyone in. It's a hard story to listen to. A collapse from civilized to beast. The narrator tells of going into the man's house after he died. He says he will never say what he saw there. It was no longer a house. It was a den. A break opens in the clouds overhead. Thick sunshine pours through the gap, a great beam of light illuminating the world in front of me. We were going to have two children. We'd take them to the park down the street to play. We'd do our best, but always know that we could have done better. They'd grow up and move away, leaving just the two of us. Two sagging collections of memories, holding hands to better brace ourselves against the hurricane of a changing world, content to let it just pass us by. She'd hold my hand while I slipped away. She'd not let go until I was gone.

The hotel in downtown Fargo is a nice one. I get checked in by 6:30. There's no message on my phone. I shower, shave, and brush my teeth. I put on my bluest pair of jeans and cleanest t-shirt. I head out the door and go outside. It's only a couple of blocks to the Sidestreet. It's a big brewpub. One whole section is taken up by a birthday party. The rest is filled by a random assortment of young and old, couples and friends. A tan girl at a table full of more of the same watches me as I come in, but quickly loses interest and looks away.

I order a beer at the bar. The beer is brewed here. They all have names related to the area. A list of inside jokes and innuendos. As I wait for my beer I look around for a face I know won't be there. The last bits of hope are shaved away. I sit at a small table by myself, drink my beer, and look at my phone. Facebook, email, CNN, and Wikipedia articles. My head raises every time somebody comes in the door. A server walks up and asks me if I could use anything. I'm hungry. Starving. I order a plate of chicken wings. BBQ. Ranch. A couple sit down at the next table over and order a plate of ribs. Two hefty people talking about nothing and giving each other shit. Two sleepy bears taking lazy swipes at each other and chuckling at each connection of paw and fur. I'm floating a bit.

The party revelers start singing happy birthday. I sing it too, quietly under my breath. The tan girl is watching the birthday party too. The beer is good. I'm definitely floating. When the server brings my chicken wings I order a second one. The two bears stop swiping at each other. They sit quiet. I can see his big paw on her considerable thigh under the table. The chicken wings aren't all that great, but they fill a hole. Tomorrow I'll be flying home. Tonight I can feel myself being lifted up into the air. The door opens, but I don't turn my head. The server brings my second beer. It tastes pretty good too.

They Should've Told You At The Door

Previously Published Works

Nickels and Dimes
First published in *Gravel*, Winter 2019

Spaghetti Sauce
First published in *Free State Review,* Issue 10, Winter 2019

Landlady
First published in *BlazeVOX*, Spring 2019

A Public Service Announcement
First published in *Ghost City Review*, Winter 2020

The Devil
First published in *Cirque Journal*, Spring 2021

They Should've Told You At The Door

Dates Written

Nickels and Dimes	December 2017
The Volunteer	June 2018
The Shadow In The Light	October 2017
Appendix	November 2016
The Devil	June 2017
Chocolates	September 2017
Centaur	March 2018
Overlook	July 2018
Siskiyou	November 2016
Date Play By Play	May 2018
The Dance	April 2018
Heil	March 2017
All You Can Eat	February 2018
The Gorge	September 2017
The Second Best Movie Review	May 2018
Misogynists and Bigots	November 2016
Landlady	February 2018
St. Paddy's Day	March 2017
Stupido	April 2017
Spaghetti Sauce	January 2018
Adventures In Dreamland With My Ex	March 2017
A Public Service Announcement	March 2018
Debate	March 2017
Totality	August 2017
It's Getting Crowded In Here	September 2017
We Hope To See Such Heights Again	December 2017
A Letter to Neal deGrasse Tyson	July 2018
Strategic Retreat	January 2018
Darkness	January 2018
Cocky Monster	February 2018
The Girl From Fargo	February 2017

Also Written By The Author

The Uncanny Valley

We all know a Paul. A person who seems to see stuff that isn't
there. The type the polite call quirky and the blunt call nuts.
Conspiracies? He's got a few. He's got his finger on how the
world really works. He knows what kind of shit is coming down
the pipe. Flee across the West Texas desert to Mexico? Makes
sense to him. Feel like you're being watched? You bet your ass
someone is watching. Best turn off your cellphone. Troubles?
Of course, that's just part of life. Doubts? No time for doubts.
Shit is getting real. Get in, buckle up, crack open a beer. The
only real question is, how far down the rabbit hole are you
willing to follow?

An Unsated Thirst

They say that an author's first stories are their most raw. Here is
a collection of S.W. Campbell's first short stories and
writings. Combining both published and unpublished works, An
Unsated Thirst explores victory and defeat, triumph and shame,
and an unflinching view of our naked selves. How one views
such stories is dependent upon the mood of the reader. Whether
we are at our highs or at our lows. However, it is hard for any of
us to claim that such stories are ones that we cannot identify
with. Contained within these pages are parts of our lives which
we try to forget, though they are an important part of what makes
us whole. Such stories should be embraced, accepted within
ourselves so we can better accept them with others.

Papaya

When a devastating hurricane hits the Caribbean island of Domenique, its inhabitants are forced into a singular struggle to survive and rebuild. Isolated in their midst is Ted, a Peace Corps volunteer who fled the ashes of his former life only to find himself labeled an outsider. Infatuated by the enigmatic wife of his only friend, Ted thrusts himself into a world beyond his comprehension. As obsession turns to desperation, tensions grow and Ted is forced to decide exactly how far he will go to rebuild amidst the muddy ruins.

Stumptown

There are places where people say things are better. Where the downtowns do not empty after dark and people dare to dream beyond their means. Quirky utopias where the sins of the past are washed away by gentle rains and we all go forward arm in arm together into the brightening sunshine. Distant locations flocked to by young pilgrims, unencumbered by the deeply driven roots of age, where everything will be different. Combining both published and unpublished work, Stumptown is a collection of stories about ordinary people, navigating their personal anxieties and drama in a time when uncertainties were still tucked away and not allowed to distort the sense of hope in the air. It is a soliloquy to naivete, and the belief that a better world is a place rather than an idea.

The People's Republic of 47th & Long

Perhaps the world would be a better place if we thought of
ourselves less as good people, and more as lousy people who
manage to do good things. My friend Leopold was always a
dreamer. The pandemic and our reactions to it left us broken and
divided. Most of us just wanted to feel safe again, but others
dreamt of something better. Leopold was one of these. Though
I think he likely joined the People's Republic of 47th and Long
purely out of geographic convenience, I know once part of it, he
fully shared in its egalitarian vision. All I have are his letters.
Sometimes I wish I had burned them, but I didn't, so now here
they are. Maybe you can find a use for them. Perhaps they can
help remind you who we truly are. The good, the bad, and most
importantly, the indifferent.

The Man In The Sodden Cap

The Man In The Sodden Cap is a collection of twenty-six short
stories written during a period of emotional unleashing, a
madcap rush to get words to the page. As with any such period
of unrelenting literary expulsion, the results are a mix of
emotional, personal, poignant, and inane. For many authors,
these are the types of stories that often get kept in a drawer
somewhere, not shared with anyone. But what use are stories if
they are not shared? Individually these are good stories, but
taken all together they tell the tale of heartbreak and remorse,
and the need to move on. In this context, The Man In A Sodden
Cap is in many ways a sequel to S.W. Campbell's first short
story collection, An Unsated Thirst, a continuation and fitting
conclusion to that earlier work.

Senseless Sensibilities

It is the human condition to try and find meaning in this life, to make sense of the chaos and randomness around us. At times this need overwhelms common sense, building layers of cognitive dissonance until we are left running our lives based upon senseless sensibilities. Contained within these pages are thirty-six short stories which explore the ability of people to adapt and survive the world around them. Stories which provide insight into slices of existence, and which highlight the strange ridiculousness of everyday life. Whether it's an old man adapting his hobbies to his aging body, a commodities trader who finds himself to be the commodity, or a lonely man fulfilling two needs in a single cross-country trip, each shows the resilience and mental flexibility shared by us all.

The Lost Art of Initial Messaging

A long time ago, before the advent of matching and swiping, online dating was largely made up of random outreach and hoped for happenstance. In this chaotic milieu, a world of nothing but shots in the dark, a charming and witty initial message could mean the difference between meeting the love of your life and sadly sitting home alone in the dark, eating lukewarm soup. Part guidebook, part memoir, and part history lesson, *The Lost Art of Initial Messaging* tracks one man's attempts to find the perfect initial message. Contained within this book are unique jewels, lovingly crafted for each prospective mate. At times poignant, at times witty, and more often than not bordering on complete ridiculousness, each represent a valiant attempt to declare: I'm here. I see you. Do you see me too?

Trials and Tribulations

A long time ago, before the advent of matching and swiping, online dating was largely made up of random outreach and hoped for happenstance. In this chaotic milieu, a world of nothing but shots in the dark, a charming and witty initial message could mean the difference between meeting the love of your life and sadly sitting home alone in the dark, eating lukewarm soup. Part guidebook, part memoir, and part history lesson, *The Lost Art of Initial Messaging* tracks one man's attempts to find the perfect initial message. Contained within this book are unique jewels, lovingly crafted for each prospective mate. At times poignant, at times witty, and more often than not bordering on complete ridiculousness, each represent a valiant attempt to declare: I'm here. I see you. Do you see me too?

More information can be found at:

www.shawnwcampbell.com

About The Author

S.W. Campbell was born in Eastern Oregon in 1983 after a harrowing drive through a fog. He currently resides in Portland, Oregon where he works as an economist and lives with a lovely house plant named Morton. He has had many short stories published in various literary reviews, some of which appear in this work, and has also self-published several books. His work can be found at www.shawnwcampbell.com.

www.ingramcontent.com/pod-product-compliance
Lightning Source LLC
Chambersburg PA
CBHW060628260626
47161CB00008B/2830

9 7 9 8 9 8 7 0 2 8 7 8 0